From Spring to Spring

From Spring to Spring

Stories of the Four Seasons

Alison Uttley

CHOSEN BY KATHLEEN LINES

illustrated by Shirley Hughes

Faber and Faber London

First published in 1978
by Faber and Faber Limited
3 Queen Square London WC1
Printed in Great Britain by
Latimer Trend & Company Ltd Plymouth

British Library Cataloguing in Publication Data

Uttley, Alison
  From spring to spring.
  I. Title II. Lines, Kathleen
  823'.9'1J   PZ7.U72

ISBN 0-571-11144-0

Contents

Foreword

Alison Uttley grew up on a steep hill-side farm in Derbyshire. The house, looking like a fortress against the sky, stood on the crest of the crag, half-encircled by a beech-wood, towering above the clustering farm buildings; a fast-flowing river ran over rocky falls in the valley below, and between was the child's world, her own private kingdom.

She knew every corner of the meadows, fields and copses. Individual trees and rocks were friendly or were strange and frightening. "A child left alone as I was, free to wander in the fields, makes her own discoveries in the world in which she lives . . . I spent most of my time seeking, hunting, pursuing the flowers, animals and butterflies, the stones and springs, the shadows and dreams of the countryside which I was making so surely my own possession." That is how, in *Ambush of Young Days*, Mrs Uttley described her own early involvement in the world of nature. And there also, and in *The Country Child*, she wrote about the excitement with which she responded to the rhythm of the year and the coming of each new month and season.

Her memories of childhood remained vivid all her life and in her stories she returned time after time to the experiences and inventions of the child she had been.

Since she felt so at one with nature, it is not surprising that in many of her fairytales the setting is out-of-doors, or that sometimes a manifestation of nature is the chief character.

The stories in *From Spring to Spring* (taken from books published during the long span of her writing life) are happy and childlike; they reveal Alison Uttley's knowledge and intuitive understanding of nature's world, and also the constant, undiminished quality of her creative imagination.

KATHLEEN LINES

Mrs Mimble and Mr Bumble Bee

In nearly the smallest house in the world lived Mrs
Mimble, a brown field-mouse. She had bright peeping
eyes and soft silky reddish hair, which she brushed and
combed each morning when she got out of bed. She was
a widow, for her husband went to market one night for
some corn, and never returned. Old Mr Toad said he
had met Wise Owl on the way. This made Mrs Mimble
nervous, and a loud sound would startle her so much
she would lock her door and go to bed.

There was only one room in the nearly-smallest house,
and that was the kitchen. Here Mrs Mimble did her
cooking and sewing, but on wash-day she rubbed her
linen in the dew and spread it out on the violet leaves to
dry. In a corner of the kitchen was a bed, and above it
ticked a dandelion clock. In another corner was a ward-
robe, and there hung her best red dress edged with fur,
and her bonnet and shawl, and the white bow she wore
on her breast.

The house was built under a hedge, among the leaves.
Its chimney reached the bottom bell of the tall foxglove,
which overshadowed the little dwelling like a great
purple tree. Mrs Mimble could put her head out of the
kitchen window and listen to the bees' orchestra in the
mottled flowers. She dearly loved a tune, and she

hummed to the bees as she went about her work. Her house was so cleverly hidden, no one would notice it. Even the tiny spiral of smoke from her chimney disappeared among the foxglove leaves like blue mist, and left only the smell of woodruff in the air.

Farther on, separated from her home by a wild-rose bush, was the very smallest house in the world.

There lived Mr Bumble Bee. He also had only one room, but it was so little, and so crowded with furniture, it was lucky he could fly, for he never could have walked through his very little door at the end of the passage.

Mr Bumble was a stout furry bee, with such a big voice that when he talked his pots rattled, and the little copper warming-pan which hung on the wall often fell down with a clatter. So he usually whispered indoors, and sang loudly when he was out in the open where nothing would be blown down. The trees and bushes were too firmly rooted for that.

He was a merry old bachelor, and it was quite natural that he and gentle Mrs Mimble should be great friends.

All through the winter the little neighbours were very quiet. Mr Bumble Bee felt so drowsy he seldom left his bed. He curled himself up in the blankets, pulled the bracken quilt over his head, and slept. His fire went out, but the door was tightly shut, and he was quite warm. Now and then he awoke and stretched his arms and legs. He fetched a little honey from his store of honey-pots in the passage and had a good meal. He drank a cup of honey-dew, and then got back to bed again.

Mrs Mimble was asleep in her house, too. The wind howled and gusts of hail beat against the door. Snow covered the ground with its deep white eiderdown and Mrs Mimble opened her eyes to look at the unexpected brightness at the small window. She jumped out of bed

and had a dinner of wheaten bread from the cupboard;
but the cold made her shiver, and she crept back under
her blankets and brown silk quilt.

Sometimes, when she felt restless, she sat in her chair,
rocking, rocking, to the scream of the north wind. Sometimes she opened the door and went out to look for holly
berries and seeds, but she never stayed long. Sometimes
she pattered to the Bumble Bee's house, but the smallest
house in the world was tightly shut, and she returned to
bed for another sleep. No smoke came from the neigh-
bouring chimneys; there were no busy marketings in the
wood and orchard, no friendly gossips on the walls. All
the very wee folk, the butterflies, bees and ants, were
resting.

One morning a bright shaft of sunlight shone straight
through the window on to the mouse's bed, and a
powder of hazel pollen blew under the door and settled
on Mrs Mimble's nose. She sneezed, Atishoo! and sprang
up.

"Whatever time is it? Have I overslept? Catkin and
pussy willow out, and I in bed?"

She washed her face in the walnut basin, and brushed
her glossy hair. Then she put on her brown dress with
the fur cuffs, and pinned a white ribbon to her breast.

"I must pop out and look at the world," said she to
herself. "Are the snowdrops over, I wonder?"

She reached down her bonnet and shawl, opened wide
her window, and set off.

Mr Bumble's door was fast shut, and although she
knocked until her knuckles were sore, no sound came
from the smallest house, and no smoke came from the
chimney.

The sun shone down and warmed Mrs Mimble's back,
and she laughed as she ran up the hill.

"Soon he will wake, and won't I tease him!" she chuckled.

She crept under a tall narrow gate into the orchard on the hillside. Over the wall hung clusters of white rock, heavy with scent, and among the flowers sang a chorus of honey-bees.

"Bumble is getting lazy," said Mrs Mimble. "He ought to be up and out now," but the bees took no notice. They were far too busy collecting honey for their hive in the corner of the orchard to listen to a field-mouse.

Under the wall was a bed of snowdrops. They pushed up their green spear-like leaves and held the white drops in veils of green gauze. Mrs Mimble wrinkled her small nose as she ran from one to another, sniffing the piercingly sweet smell of spring. In a corner a company of flowers was out, wearing white petticoats and green embroidered bodices. Mrs Mimble sat up on her hind legs and put out a paw to stroke them. The bells shook at her gentle touch, and rang a peal, "Ting-a-ling-spring-a-ling."

She turned aside and ran up the high wall to the white rock and gathered a bunch for Mr Bumble Bee, to the honey-bees' annoyance.

"Let him get it himself," they grumbled.

Then down she jumped, from stone to stone, and hunted for coltsfoot in the orchard to make herb-beer.

Time had slipped away, and the sun was high when she neared home. A fine smoke, which only her sharp eyes could spy, came from Mr Bumble's chimney. The door was wide open, and a crackly sound and a loud Hum-m-m-m came from within as the Bumble Bee cleaned his boots and chopped the sticks.

There was no doubt Mr Bumble was very wide awake, but whether it was through Mrs Mimble knocking at the door, or spring rapping at the window, nobody knows.

As Mrs Mimble stood hesitating, a three-legged stool, an arm-chair, and a bed came hurtling through the air and fell on the gorse bush, over the way.

"There it goes! Away it goes! And that! And that!" shouted Mr Bumble, and the warming-pan and the kettle followed after.

"Whatever are you doing, Mr Bumble?" exclaimed Mrs. Mimble, now thoroughly alarmed.

"Oh, good day, Mrs Mimble. A Happy New Year to you," said the Bee, popping a whisker round the door. "I'm spring-cleaning. There isn't room to stir in this house until I've emptied it. I am giving it a good turn-out," and a saucepan and fiddle flew over the Mouse's head.

"It's a fine day for your spring-cleaning," called Mrs Mimble, trying to make her high little squeak heard over the Buzz-Buzz, Hum, Hum, Hum-m-m, and the clatter of dishes and furniture.

"Yes, Buzz! Buzz! It is a fine day. I think I slept too long, so I'm making up for lost time."

"Lost thyme, did you say! It isn't out yet, but white rock is, and I have brought you some." She laid her bunch near his door.

But when a table crashed down on her long slender tail, she fled past the gorse bush where the bed lay among the prickles, past the rose bush where the fiddle and warming-pan hung on the thorns, to her own little house. She pushed open the door and sank on a chair.

"Well, I never!" she cried. "I'm thankful to get safely here, and more than thankful that rose bush is between my house and Mr Bumble's! His may be the tiniest house in all the world, it is certainly the noisiest!"

She looked round her kitchen, and for the first time noticed a cobweb hanging from the ceiling, and drifted leaves and soil on her grass-woven carpet.

Up she jumped and seized a broom. Soon she was as busy as Mr Bumble. She hung out the carpet on a low branch of the rose-tree to blow in the wind and she scrubbed her floor. She swept the walls, and hung fresh white curtains at the window, where they fluttered like flower-petals. She festooned her blankets on the bushes, and wound up the dandelion clock, and polished her table and chairs. She made the teapot shine like a moonbeam.

All the time she could hear a loud Hum-Hum-Boom-Boom-Buzz coming from over the rose bush, and a bang and clatter as knives, forks, and spoons flew about.

When she had finished her work, and her house smelled of wild-thyme soap, and lavender polish, Bumble Bee was collecting his possessions from the gorse bush and rose bush where they had fallen.

"Boom! Boom! Buzz! Help me, Mrs Mimble!" he called, and she ran outside and sat with little paws held up, and her bright eyes inquiring what was the matter.

"I've lost a spoon, my honey-spoon. It has a patent handle to keep it from falling in the honey-pot, and now I've lost it," and he buzzed up and down impatiently, seeking among the spiny branches of the rose bush.

Mrs Mimble looked among the brown leaves of the foxglove, but it wasn't there. She turned over the violet leaves, and peeped among the green flowers of the Jack-by-the-hedge, and ran in and out of the gorse bush, but still she could not find it.

It was lost, and Mr Bumble grumbled so loudly that a passer-by exclaimed: "It is really spring! Listen to the bees humming!"

Except for the loss of his spoon Mr Bumble was perfectly happy, and his friend, Mrs Mimble, was so merry it was a joy to be near her. Although she was too large to enter his house, he used to visit hers, and many an evening they spent before her open window, eating honey and wheat biscuits, and sipping nectar as they listened to the song of the bees. Each day was a delight to these little field-people.

One morning the Mouse knocked on Mr Bumble's door and called to him to come out.

"I have some news, Mr Bumble, some news! I've found a nest to let," she cried.

Mr Bumble was resting after a long flight across the Ten-Acre Field, but he put down his newspaper and flew to the door.

"A nest? What do you want with a nest?" he asked.

"It's a chaffinch's nest, a beautiful old one, lined with the very best hair and wool. It will make a summer-house, where I can go for a change of air now and then."

"Shall we both go and see it?" asked the Bee, kindly.

Mrs Mimble ran home and put on her best red dress with fur edging, and her brown bonnet and shawl in honour of the occasion. The Bee combed his hair and brushed his coat with the little comb and brush he carried in his trouser pocket.

They walked down the lane together, but soon Mr Bumble was left behind. He was such a slow walker, and Mrs Mimble was so nimble, she ran backwards and forwards in her excitement, urging him on.

"Come on, Mr Bumble. Hurry up, Mr Bee," she cried.

"It's this dust that gets on my fur," said the Bee. "Besides, you must remember that my legs are shorter than yours."

He puffed and panted and scurried along, but Mrs Mimble was impatient.

"Can't you fly?" she asked.

"Oh, yes, I can fly," he replied, ruffled because he wished to try to walk with her. He shook the dust from his legs, and with a deep Hum-m-m-m he soared up into the air. Higher and higher he flew, into the branches of the beech-tree, where he buzzed among the long golden buds with their tips of green.

"Now he's gone, and I have offended him," said the Mouse, ruefully. She sat sadly on a daisy tuffet, with her tearful eyes searching among the trees for her friend. At length she spied him, swinging on a twig, fluttering like a goldfinch on a thistle.

"Come down, Mr Bumble, come down," she piped in her wee shrill voice. "I will run, and you shall fly just over my head, then we shall arrive together. And I do think you are a splendid pedestrian for your size."

Mrs Mimble looked so pathetic and small down there under the great trees, that he relented and flew down to her. He was flattered too at the long word she had used. So they travelled, great friends again, along the lane, under the hedge of thorn and ash, she running in and out of the golden celandines and green fountains of Jack-by-the-hedge, he buzzing and singing and sipping the honey as he flew near.

When they reached the thickest part of the hedge, she ran up a stout hawthorn bush, and leaped into a small oval nest which had a label "To LET" nailed to it by a large thorn.

"Isn't it a perfect house, with a view, too!" said the Mouse, waving her paw to the hills far away.

The Bee perched near on a bough, and swayed backwards and forwards with admiration. The nest was green and silver with moss and lichen, delicate as a mistletoe bunch. Its roof was open to the stars, but an overhanging mat of twigs and leaves kept out the rain. All that Mrs

Mimble needed was a coverlet, and then she could sleep, lulled by the wind.

"I shall bring my brown silk quilt and keep it here, for no one will take it, it's just like a dead leaf. When I want a change of air, I shall come for a day or two, and live among the may blossom."

They agreed she should take possession at once.

Mr Bumble, whose handwriting was neat, wrote another notice, and pinned it to the tree, for all to read who could.

Mrs Mimble
Her House
Private

The very next day she came with the brown silk quilt, and her toothbrush and comb packed in a little bag. The Bee sat outside his own small house, and waved a red handkerchief to her.

"Good-bye. I will keep the robbers from your home," he called, and he locked her door and put the key in his pocket.

Mrs Mimble climbed up to her summer-house, and leaned from the balcony to watch the life below.

Ants scurried along the grass, dragging loads of wood for their stockades. Sometimes two or three carried a twig, or a bundle of sticks. One little ant dropped his log down a hole, and all his efforts could not move it. As he pulled and tugged a large ant came up and boxed his ears for carelessness. Then he seized the wood and took it away himself to the Ant Town.

"A shame! A shame!" called Mrs Mimble. "It's the little fellow's log. He found it," but no one took any notice, and the small weeping ant dried his tears on the leaves.

Then Mrs Mimble heard a tinkle of small voices, and a lady-bird came by with her five children dressed in red spotted cloaks.

"How many legs has a caterpillar got, Mother?" inquired a tiny voice, but the mother hurried along, and then flew up in the air with the children following, and Mrs Mimble, who nearly fell out of her nest as she watched them, never heard the answer.

"I will ask Mr Bumble," said she. "He knows everything."

Two beetles swaggered up and began to fight. They rose on their hind legs and cuffed and kicked each other. They circled round and round one another, with clenched fists and glaring eyes.

"It's mine. I found it," said one beetle, swinging out his arm.

"Take that, and that!" shouted the other, boxing with both arms at once, and dancing with rage. "I saw it fall, and I had it first."

"I carried it here," said the first beetle, parrying the blows.

Mrs Mimble glanced round, and there, on a wide-open dandelion lay a tiny gleaming spoon—Bumble Bee's honey-spoon with the patent handle.

Softly she ran down the tree, and silently she slipped under the shelter of the jagged dandelion leaves, and put the spoon in her pocket. Then she returned as quietly as she had come, and still the beetles banged and biffed each other, shouting: "It's mine."

At last, tired out, they sat down for a minute's rest, and lo! the treasure was gone! Whereupon they scurried here and there, hunting in the grass, till Mrs Mimble lost sight of them.

She put on her bonnet, intending to run home with the find, when she heard the loud Zoom! Buzz! Buzz! of her friend, and the Bumble Bee came blundering along in a zig-zag path, struggling to carry a long bright object on his back.

"I thought the new house might be damp," he panted, bringing the copper warming-pan from across his wing, "for no one has slept in it since the chaffinches were here last spring."

"Oh, Mr Bumble, how kind you are! How thoughtful!" exclaimed the Mouse. She rubbed the warming-pan, which contained an imprisoned sunbeam, over the downy nest and drove out the little damps.

"Now I have something for you," she continued, and she took from her pocket the honey-spoon, the small spoon as big as a daisy petal with its patent handle and all.

The sun came out from behind a round cloud, the small leaves packed in their sheaths moved and struggled to get out. Mrs Mimble heard the sound of the million buds around her, whispering, uncurling, and flinging away their wraps as they peeped at the sun. She leaned from her balcony and watched the crowds of field creatures, snails and ants, coming and going in the grassy streets below.

But restless Mr Bumble flew away for his fiddle, away across the field and along the lane to his own smallest house. He tuned the little fiddle, and dusted it, and held it under his wide chin. Then he settled himself on a bough near his dear friend, and played the song of the Fairy Etain, who was changed into a bee, in Ireland, a thousand years ago, but has always been remembered in legend and verse by the bees themselves.

The gentle Mouse sat listening to his tiny notes, sweet as honey, golden as the sunlight overhead, and she was glad, for she knew that summer was not far away.

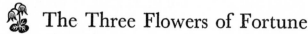 The Three Flowers of Fortune

One fine day in spring, when the orchards were full of apple blossom, and the lambs were playing in the meadows, a little girl named Sally Thorne ran out of her mother's cottage. She skipped between the lavender bushes, and through the wicket gate, to the field at the bottom of the garden. The grass was full of flowers, daisies and primroses, violets and bluebells, but Sally liked the daisies best of all. She gathered a tight little bunch and every flower had a circle of frilly white petals round a yellow face. Among them she found one with two heads. Fancy that! Two heads on one stalk! There never was such a strange happening before in all Sally's life, for everyone knows a daisy has only one head.

Sally raced back to her mother, up the garden, and in at the door. Mrs Thorne was busy with her arms in the wash-tub, washing the clothes for the Big House up on the hill.

"Mother! Mother! Look! I've found a daisy with two heads growing on one stalk! What does that mean, Mother?" cried Sally, holding out her double flower.

Her mother put down the sheet she was washing, wiped the suds from her hands, and took the daisy. She held it up to the sunlight, and twirled it round.

"Well I never!" she exclaimed. "A daisy with two heads! I don't know what it foretells, child, but it must have some meaning. I will show it to the lady's maid at the Big House, for she is very clever."

She put the daisy in water on the window-sill, and went on with her washing, but Sally peered at it and wondered about it all day long.

The next day Sally ran out to the little field to pick a bunch of clover. There was a fine clover bed, humming with bees, and the smell was so sweet she wrinkled her nose and lay on her face to get close to the flowers. As she picked the red and white spiky balls, and tasted the honey which lies deep inside them, she noticed a strange thing. There was a four-leaved clover growing among the others. Everybody knows a clover has only three leaflets, and here was one with four! It was a miracle, Sally thought, and she gathered the leaf and put it in with her bunch of flowers.

She ran back to her mother, across the grass and through the lavender hedge, shouting: "Mother! Mother! Look!" as she waved her four-leaved clover to her mother, who was busy ironing the clothes and hanging them round the fire.

"Mother! I've found a four-leaved clover! What does it mean?"

Mrs Thorne put down the shirt she was ironing, and replaced the iron by the fire. Then she took the clover-leaf to the window, and looked at it.

"Well I never!" she cried. "A four-leaved clover! Three-leaved clover is the sign of the Trinity, I learned at school, but whatever can a four-leaved clover mean? I must take it to the lady's maid when I go up to the Big House with the laundry. Maybe she can tell me the meaning," and she put the clover-leaf in water alongside the daisy.

The next day Sally ran out to the field to pick a bunch of bluebells. They grew close under the wall, so blue that they looked as if a bit of the sky had fallen down, or a pool of water lay there. She snapped the brittle stalks, and filled her small hot hands, and each flower seemed to tinkle its bells at her, and each flower seemed to be larger than the one before. Just as she was going away she found a white bluebell, growing apart from the others, pure and snowy in the deep green grass.

She scampered home, carrying her bunch of sweet-scented bluebells, and among them the flower with its bells like pearls. She hurried through the wicket gate, and up the stony path, to her mother who was baking in the kitchen.

"Mother! Mother! Look what I've found! A white bluebell! What does it mean, Mother?"

Mrs Thorne wiped the dough from her hands, and picked up the bluebell. It really was a wonderful flower!

"Well I never!" cried she. "I'm sure I don't know what it means, but it must have some reason for growing this colour, when it ought to be blue. I'll take it up to the Big House tomorrow, and then I shall find out. The lady's maid is a friend of mine, and she'll tell me."

So she put the white bluebell with the four-leaved clover and the double-headed daisy on the window-sill, and went on with her baking, and Sally had to be content.

The next day Mrs Thorne packed all the washing in a basket and put it on a wheelbarrow. On the top of the cloth lay the three flowers. She wheeled her burden up the drive, and turned aside to the back door, behind the kitchen garden.

"Look what my little girl found in our field!" she said to the lady's maid, as she sipped a cup of tea before going back. "What do you make of these? All three growing in our field. None of them ordinary, you see."

The lady's maid was a clever young woman, who came from a big town. She had been to school in a great red-brick building, with inspectors popping in and out of the doors, and certificates awarded once a year. She knew all kinds of things, but she didn't know the meaning of the double-headed daisy, the four-leaved clover, and the white bluebell.

"I'll show them to the governess," said she. "She is certain to know."

The governess was a high-born young lady who had studied nearly everything. She had been to college, and knew about flowers and their insides, and even about their thoughts. There was nothing she did not know, till she saw the double-headed daisy, the four-leaved clover, and the white bluebell, but she did not know what they meant.

"These are extraordinary botanical specimens," said she. "I do not remember the exact significance of their queerness, but I will ask her ladyship."

Her ladyship was walking in the garden, and the governess took the flowers out to her at once.

But her ladyship did not know either. She had spent her childhood in foreign countries, and she could speak five languages, but she could not tell the meaning of the double-headed daisy, the four-leaved clover, and the white bluebell.

In the garden bed a short distance away a young boy was weeding. He was Tom Thatcher, the fourth gardener's assistant. He heard the conversation between the governess and her ladyship, and he saw the three flowers in their hands, so he upped and spoke.

"Please, your ladyship, and please, miss," said he, pulling his forelock. "Please, I knows what them flowers means. Please, they means: 'Good Luck and God Bless you,' for whosumdever finds them. That's what they mean, your ladyship and miss, if you'll excuse me."

And he blushed for his boldness, pulling his forelock again, and returning to his weeding.

So the governess told the lady's maid, and the lady's maid told Sally's mother, and she told her young daughter.

"Good Luck and God Bless you," whispered Sally to herself, and she hid the words in her heart.

But when Sally was grown up she married the fourth gardener's assistant, for he had become the head-gardener, and he was her luck.

🌼 Green Shoes

Underneath the hedge lay an old pair of shoes. The toes were broken, and the soles nearly parted from the uppers. The laces had long ago decayed, and the tongue was a ragged scrap of wet leather. They had lain there among the dog mercury and Robin-run-in-the-hedge for many a long month. They had been hidden under snow, and rimed with the frost, and soaked with winter storms, and now they were lost in the hedgebottom, as much a part of it as the ferns and velvety moss and young leaves. Soil was washed into the cracks, and moss took root there and grew with feathery tufts and pearly beads. Little ferns of exquisite shape sprang up and waved their green fronds from the soles. Seeds of tiny plants dropped from above and after the sun had shone little red and blue flowers came out where the tongue should have been. Very soon the shoes would have disappeared altogether, and become absorbed in the green mat of Mother Earth, but before they were completely changed they were discovered.

An old man walked down that green lane, and a very ancient man he was. He had a store of knowledge and a power of wisdom remembered from other days. He carried a sack on his bent back, and he stooped so low he almost touched the ground with his beard as he went along the leafy way. His eyes missed nothing, not a pearly-striped snail-shell, or a mailed beetle, not a moth with folded wings, or an ant busy with its citizen's work. He stayed to watch one of these little creatures carrying a log twice its own size, and he nodded his head to it and whispered a word of encouragement. Then he spoke to a butterfly, and the insect flew upon his hand and kissed him with soft kisses. He talked to the booming bumble bee, and touched the warm furry body, and the bee's voice was quiet as it listened. Then away it went, deep in the flowers' honeybags. He gave a greeting to the Lords and Ladies in their green voluminous gowns, and they threw wide their cloaks and bowed their brown heads to his words. Evidently he was somebody whom they all knew very well indeed.

"If only mankind would listen to the talk of the country lanes, they would forget their cares and find that peace of mind which they seem to have lost," murmured the old man, as he stroked the brown sleek head of a robin. The robin flicked its tail and cocked its head aside in a knowing way, and flew straight as an arrow to tell the student at his desk what it had heard. The student went on reading, and although the bird sang with all its might he took no notice at all.

Down in the hedgerow the ancient one had spied the pair of old shoes. He leaned over them and contemplated them for many minutes, and then he made a sign over them. He spoke a word of an old forgotten language, and then he trudged away down the lane, bestowing the kind glances of his brown eyes on the humble creatures of earth, whispering a word of cheer, helping a hurt one, bringing the balm of forgetfulness to another, praising flowers and birds and insects.

B

From that moment the shoes were enchanted. Ferns and moss and many coloured flowers were woven into a living tissue, strong as leather, supple as silk. Immortal powers were breathed into them. They lay under the hedgerow a pair of magical shoes. They were found a few days later by Tom Gratton the farm labourer as he went home from his ditching and hedging.

He picked them up and examined them in wonder. He saw a pair of green shoes, made of painted leather, soft as velvet, with red and yellow flowers on the tongues and laces made of rainbow gossamer. The lining was of thistledown fur, silver-white. The soles were made of growing moss. Never were seen such dainty shoes! He wrapped them in his red spotted pocket-handkerchief, which had held his dinner basin, and he carried them home to his daughter Milly.

They fitted her slim little feet as if they had been made for her. Milly had only worn heavy nailed boots, iron-tipped and harsh to her toes, and these were soft and warm, light as a feather, and a joy to look upon.

"Oh, look at me! I'm a lady! Oh! Can I wear them to go to school to-morrow? I want to show them to the other girls!" she cried, dancing across the kitchen like a kitten at play, and the shoes seemed to spin her round.

"Well, they aren't really suitable for school, but you can wear them to-morrow, my poppet," said her doting mother, smiling at the little girl's happy face.

So Milly went to school in the fairy shoes. At least she started for school, on that fine morning in spring. How the children stared! "Green shoes! Green shoes!" they mocked enviously, but Milly danced down the village street, willy-nilly, where the shoes took her. The school-bell jangled in the little tower, the boys and girls trooped into the classroom, but Milly didn't appear.

"Her's gone off down th' Fox's Hollow," cried a little boy. "Her's playing truant, is Milly Gratton."

"In a pair of lovely shoes, green velvet," added a little girl.

But Milly wasn't playing truant. The shoes were taking her to the places they knew, where the moss was thick and clubbed with golden seeds, and the lichens starred the stones, and little red and yellow flowers sprang from cushions of tiny plants. Her eyes opened wider than ever as she saw all the beauties which had been invisible to her before. There she stayed, listening to the talk of the finches, the whispering chatter of insects, the deep wisdom of the rustling trees, and there her father found her at nightfall when the whole village had been searching for her.

The pretty green shoes were taken off and wiped dry, and Milly was sent to bed with a basin of bread and milk for supper. She told her mother and father she had been by the side of the ditch hearing the talk of the rushes, and the gossip of the little yellow frogs. She had watched the spider spin its silken web, and heard the creak of the threads as they rubbed the twigs. Quite plain to her had been the mumble of flies, and the whir of wings and feathers, and the swish of the butterfly's wings.

Her poor parents shook their heads at her, and fetched the wise woman.

"Yes, she must stay a-bed and drink camomile tea," said the wise woman.

She picked up the green shoes which lay by the side of the bed, and turned them over and smelled at their sweetness.

"Shoes too fine for the child to wear on weekdays," said she disapprovingly. "She's got a chill with wearing them down in that ditch. If you want her to keep sensible, you must put aside these till Sundays. Let her go to church in them and nowhere else. Let her go to Holy Church."

On Sunday Milly was dressed in her Sunday frock, her Sunday tippet and Sunday gloves, and best hat. On her feet she wore the green shoes, with their silky laces and flowery tongues. As she went up the churchyard, under the yew trees, the shoes gave a tug at her feet. They twisted her right round, and away they ran with her, away from the parson and the choir-boys and the pealing bells. Away they ran, as fast as they could patter, and they never stopped till they came to the green lane where the Lords and Ladies stood in their green cloaks. "Jack-in-the-pulpit" was the Sunday name of the flowers, and they preached a sermon to Milly in her green shoes.

So Milly sat down in the hedgebottom, and rested her little feet, while she listened to the words of the brown preachers in their green pulpits among the flowers and leaves. The birds sang the psalms, the chiff-chaff sang a

hymn, and all the tiny creatures of the lane with the trees above and the flowers below chanted praises to God. Far away the church bells rang in vain for Milly. The only bells she could hear were the bluebells swinging their chimes and the Alleluia flowers shaking their delicate heads close to the ground.

After a time Milly got drowsy with the music around her, the singing and the chanting of the wild world. She leaned over the little brook and listened to the reedy talk of the fish. She untied the gossamer laces and stripped off her shoes and stockings and dipped her feet in the water, intent on hearing the talk down below. The fish had scales of silver and green, they stared with unwinking eyes and opened and shut their mouths in amazement at the tale their brother was telling. It was a magical tale of a mermaid who lived at the bottom of the sea. On and on went the story, and some said they didn't believe it, and others swore it was true. Milly bent her head low till her dark locks touched the water. The voices were suddenly hushed, and the fish no longer talked. She could only hear the murmur of the stream as it fell over the stones and the singing of the birds in the overhanging trees. She stepped to the bank, but her green shoes were gone. They had floated away down that little stream, and although Milly hunted for many a day in the meadows and ditches, they had gone for ever.

But they had left a memory behind them, and Milly never forgot the lessons they taught her when she wore them that Sunday morning.

In the meantime the shoes were carried by the current to a small brook that flowed into the millpond. The green shoes were caught among the water-lily leaves in the silent pool off the mill-race. Little Jack Peter saw them and he ran to the shed for his fishing net.

"Here's a fine catch," he cried, as he drew them from the water. "A pair of shoes, quite good ones, and the wet hasn't even got inside them. Lined with fur, and all painted and broidered in colours! Oh my! Perhaps they will fit my mother!"

The miller and his wife rejoiced over the pretty shoes, and when the good woman tried them on they fitted her perfectly. It was part of their magical power to fit anyone who tried them on. They never ran away with her, for she lived in the green lanes. They took her to the orchard drying ground with her linen basket, to the field to feed the hens, to the garden to pick the herbs to stuff the fish for dinner, and they always behaved in the most decorous manner.

Her eyes were brightened, she saw many a thing unseen before, but she was wise enough to say nothing to others. She stored the marvels in her mind, and told the tales of them to little Jack Peter. Every day she told him a new story, and nobody knew where she got them all from.

One day the shoes were set neatly side by side in their usual place underneath the kitchen dresser, when a tramp pushed open the door and saw them. Quickly he picked them up and popped them in his pocket. Then away he sidled before even the dog could bark or the gander give a warning cry.

The poor miller's wife burst into tears for her loss, but her husband tried to console her.

"They came by mystery, and by mystery they've gone away, so don't 'ee take on, my love."

" 'Twas no mystery. 'Twas an old bad tramp as took 'em, I'm sure certain," she exclaimed, but there was no getting the shoes back again.

However, in a few months' time a little daughter was

born to her, and the child shared Jack Peter's delight in the magical tales the miller's wife told them.

The tramp carried away the dainty shoes. He wandered along country lanes and slept in ditches and cooked his dinner and boiled his billy-can under the hedges. He thought he would never get to the town, for while he had the green shoes in his pocket every road took him away. Finally he arrived, and he tossed the shoes on the wooden counter of a little cobbler's shop.

"How much for these? High-class shoes, come from a palace, I 'specks," said he.

"I'll give you a shilling for them," said the cobbler sternly, "and not a penny more, for it's my belief you've not come by them honestly."

So the tramp had to part with them for a shilling. The cobbler put them in his window with a fair price on them. They were strange shoes. They made his fingers tingle when he held them, and he heard bells ringing and he smelled meadow-sweet and honeysuckle and he heard little voices calling in the wainscot where the mice lived. He was glad to get rid of the green shoes to a young man who entered the shop and asked about the pair of strange outlandish shoes with their tongues of flowers and their gossamer laces.

He wanted them for his sweetheart. He called her his sweetheart, but she would have nothing to do with him. She was a dancer at the theatre in the town. He was a poet, but he had written nothing for weeks. Every night he sat at the back of the theatre, in the cheapest seat, and he craned his head to watch those little twinkling feet, and the sparkling eyes of his beloved. She had danced away with his heart and left him with an empty space. He thought that if he gave her the lovely green shoes she might smile on him and give him her heart in exchange.

So he carried the shoes home to his lodging and put them down by the side of the empty grate while he wrote a letter. Even as the pen scratched the paper he was disturbed by soft movements, rustling whispers. The shoes were feathery with growing ferns, and the flowers embroidered upon them were opening new buds. He stooped down and slipped his hands into them, and the warmth of the growing things seemed to fill his chilled body. His cramped fingers took up the pen again, and he began to write. The pen flew over the paper, as if invisible fingers guided it. The warmth spread through his body. Something had happened to him. He wrote on and on, aware only of the scent of wild flowers, the humming of bees and the song of birds. He seemed to be in a leafy lane again, under the hedgerow, filled with the delight of his native country.

He looked at the shoes, and they were covered with growing flowers and delicate young leaves. He looked at his words, and it wasn't a letter at all that he had written. It was a poem, the outpouring of his soul. The words burned him. He was no longer lonely or sad. He forgot the dancer and the theatre and the poverty of the town. He held the green shoes to his heart, and he went on writing till dawn.

The next day he sent the shoes to the dancer. At night she danced so divinely in the soft flowery shoes that everyone said they had never seen the like. She was a ballerina, a star, a genius. At the back of the theatre sat the poet, and the dancer smiled at him, and kissed her hand to him alone when the house applauded her.

She came dancing through the streets with the green shoes on her dainty feet and the poet took her away to the countryside. There in the lane they told their love, and they hung the shoes in the hedge.

They sat on a cushion of Queen Anne's Lace, violets and rosy campions, and the poet read his poem.

They vowed to love each other for ever, the poet who had written his greatest poem, and the little actress who had danced her finest dance. When they stood up the little shoes had gone. That didn't matter. They went back without them and bought another pair, not so pretty but quite useful. When people are deep in love shoes do not matter.

The little green shoes had fallen in the ditch once more and there they lay, growing even more beautiful in the sun and rain, till they were found by a gypsy with a roving eye and jet black hair.

He held them up aloft and sang with joy, for he knew what he would do with them. He went back to the painted caravan for his piebald pony. He flung himself on its back and rode off to the castle, where the lovely young bride had lately come. He rang the iron bell at the great door, and asked to see the lady.

"My lady is not at home to a gypsy fellow," said the man-servant, and he shut the door.

Out of the window peeped the lady herself, in her blue silk dress and her green silk hood.

"Shoes for sale. Fine shoes for sale," called the gypsy, holding the delicate shoes aloft, and standing up on the pony's back.

She stretched out a white hand and took them and tossed down her purse of gold, but the gypsy threw a flaming kiss to burn her.

She ran back to her room and slipped the shoes on her feet. How beautiful they were! How gay she felt! Never in all her dull, short, married life had she felt such happiness.

She leaned out of the window and the gypsy still waited.

"I'm coming with you!" she whispered. "Will you have me?"

"Most willingly," he laughed back to her.

She tore off her gold ring; she changed her silken dress; she wrapped a scarf round her curls and draped a cloak on her shoulders. "Tell my lord I'm off with the gypsies," said she to her maid, and away she went.

Ah! How the green shoes danced that night! How they flashed in and out of the firelight, as my lady swung round in the arms of the dark gypsy man. And when the fire burned low, and the gypsies slept under the stars, the little green shoes lay tossed in the gorse bush where the lady dropped them with her cloak and dress.

Deep into the yellow gorse they fell, and nobody missed them when the gypsies went away to a new camping-ground the next day. The lady rode on the piebald pony, and the gypsy ran by her side, holding her bridle, whispering to her, enchanting her ears, and no one saw the little green shoes in the gorse bush.

There they lie, waiting for another wearer, for they are immortal shoes, and who knows who will find them next?

The Rainbow

Tom Oliver had been fishing all the morning in the little brook which ran down the fields—the silver shining brook which rattled over the stones, grinding them into pebbles, the stream which seized the meadow grasses and dragged them by their green hair, so that they looked like water-nymphs, swimming in the rapid little torrent.

Tadpoles and minnows and Jack Sharps were the only creatures that lived there, for the brook was so noisy that the big fish preferred to swim in the quiet river lower down the valley. Tom's mother would not allow him to go near the deep pools and hollows of that tranquil water, but when he leaned over the humpbacked bridge, with his face half-buried in the ferns on the edge, he could watch the dark slim shapes mysteriously moving down below, and sometimes he saw a real fisherman in waders standing in the water, and landing a speckled trout.

But the brook was a splendid place for a boy's fishing. The quickest way to catch anything was to dangle an empty jampot in the water, or to dip a brown hand under a stone, although Tom preferred to do it properly, and to use a fishing rod made of a hazel switch, with a bit of string on the end, and almost anything for bait—a holly berry, a cherry, an acorn.

He was fishing like this, sitting cross-legged on a stone under an alder-tree, and the sun was shining brightly, so that spickles and sparkles of light flashed about on the water, and flickering nets of sunshine lay on the bottom of the brook. Suddenly he felt a bite, and the cherry bobbed and dipped as if something very much alive was on the end.

Quickly he pulled in his line, and there, wriggling on the end, was no minnow, or Jack Sharp, or Miller's thumb, but a rainbow, a curving iridescent rainbow, with all the seven lovely colours in its arching back. It leaped and danced on its tail so that Tom had much to do to catch it.

It was quite a little rainbow when Tom carried it home, all writhing and slipping in his fingers, but when he put it in the garden, it grew so large that it stretched across from the lilac bush to the silver birch-tree, in a beautiful curving sweep of misty colours. He could no longer hold it, for it slithered through his hands like dew-drops, but there it hung, in a fine archway, a marvel for all the world to see.

Tom's mother left her wash-tub, and stood at the kitchen door for a moment.

"Yes, it's a rainbow, right enough," said she. "I've never seen a rainbow in our garden before. It cheers one up to see it," and she went back to her work.

Tom spent all day looking at his rainbow, running his fingers through its elusive colour bands, catching the blue and orange in his hands. The chaffinches fluttered through it, and the tom tits swung on the top, as if it were a bough of a celestial tree, so that their wings were flecked with many lights.

A blackbird whistled at the foot where the arch rested on the lilac-tree, and a thrush sang at the other end, on

the silver birch. All the birds saw the rainbow hanging
in the garden, and they called to one another to play in
and out of the great arch.

"It would make a nice clothes' line," said Tom's
mother, thoughtfully, and she carried out the washing-
basket and started to peg the shirts and towels on the
bands of colour. But they slipped through and fell to the
ground, and the rainbow shook itself so that drops of
water sprinkled them like rain. With a sigh Mrs Oliver

gathered them up and took them to the drying-ground.
It was a pity she could not make use of such a nice
clean rope of colour, for it was a pretty sight.

The curious thing about it was that some other people
could not see it. Cross Mr Jenkins, the chimney-sweep
next door, saw nothing at all. Mrs Stone, who kept the
little grocery store in her front window, saw nothing
either, although she put on her spectacles and peered
quite close, but little Jemima Stone could see it, and she
came into the garden and stood with Tom Oliver, watching the rainbow's twinkling colours, which changed as
the children moved.

Night came, but still the rainbow glowed in the garden.
Tom's mother said it would disappear when the sun set,
and certainly even Tom's sharp eyes couldn't see it in the
dark, but when he moved his fingers across it he could
feel it like a ripple in the air, and he knew it was there.

The stars came out, and the moon rose above the hill.
Tom leaned from his bedroom window, and looked down
to the garden. Yes, the bow was still there, with strange
pale colours of silver, and on the highest point of the arch
a nightingale perched itself and sang its haunting
passionate song. That was indeed a sight to remember!

The next morning when Tom sprang from bed and
poked his head out of the casement the first thing he
saw was the rainbow, all fresh and bright, swinging
lightly across the garden. So it hadn't gone! Surely
somebody would see it to-day! He wanted to share the
good news with all the village.

He ran off to school with his bag flapping on his back,
eager to tell his friends about it.

"We've got a rainbow in our back garden," he
boasted.

"Don't believe you," said one.

"Rainbows don't belong to gardens," said another.

"You come home with me, and I'll show you," said Tom.

When the boys followed him through the garden gate they said there was nothing there, and mocked at Tom.

"It's hanging in the lilac-tree. Can't you see it? Can't you see it? You must all be blind," said Tom, exasperated, and he put his head on one side and pointed out the lovely colours spanning the trees in the airy filmy archway.

"Oh leave him! It's all nonsense! There's no rainbow! Leave him to his moonshine," they exclaimed, and off they ran to look for birds' nests in the hedges.

Tom hung his head and walked into the house. Only his mother and little Jemima Stone could see the rainbow. What was the good of it if nobody believed in it? Perhaps it wasn't there at all, and he had imagined it. He ran to the door and looked out, and was just in time to see the rainbow rapidly growing smaller. It curled into a little ball and fell in a wreath of colour to the ground.

Although he hunted and hunted he couldn't find it. He searched among the cabbages, the carrots, and onions, but there was no rainbow. He looked among the pansies, the sweet-williams and bachelor's buttons, but there was no sign of a rainbow among the flowers. Where could it have gone? He turned sadly away, unhappy that he had doubted and so lost his treasure, when a sparkle on the rubbish heap caught his eye. He picked up a little prism of glass, and held it to the sun. Bands of coloured light fell from it, and he shouted with joy.

"I've caught the rainbow again, Mother. It's shut up in this glass, like a ship in a bottle!"

He turned it this way and that and let the spectrum of colour fall on his hands.

"Where was it, Tom?" asked Mrs Oliver, running to the door.

"On the rubbish heap. Look at it, all the colours, and not one missing. Violet, indigo, blue, green, yellow, orange, red. All of them, fast in the glass."

"It can't escape me this time," he continued, twirling the prism. "I can take it to school, and the boys must believe me."

He put the prism from the chandelier in his pocket and ran laughing down the lane, and when he showed it to the other boys they all agreed they could see the rainbow now.

But his mother returned to her wash-tub, and bent over the clothes. There, dancing over the soap-suds, glimmering in the bubbles, were a thousand little rainbows of light.

"I've got a bit of that rainbow, too," she told herself. "Once I thought it lived in the sky, and now I've seen it even in my old wash-tub. Who would believe it?" She took up her soap and rubbed the clothes, and then she began to sing with happiness.

🌿 The Cornfield

It was a warm, sweet-scented summer evening, and the moon and a few stars shone down on the fields, which lay like sheets of pale silver on the hillside. A hedgehog jogged along the country lane between the hedges, singing to himself his own little song of happiness.

> *My lantern's the moon,*
> *My candle's a star,*
> *I travel by night,*
> *I wander afar.*

He stamped his small feet in the dust in time to his thin high voice, and he felt the cool air in his prickles. A nightingale sang in the wood, but the hedgehog took no notice of its passionate music. He went on with his own song, singing so softly nobody but himself could hear it.

> *My carpet's the moss,*
> *My firelight the sun,*
> *My house-roof the hedge,*
> *When work is all done.*

It was a good song, he told himself, a traveller's song, and he was a hedgehog who couldn't abide staying at home. All day he had slept in his little bed of leaves, under the hedge, warmed by the hot sun, sheltered by tall ferns and velvety moss. Now night had come, and, in common with many small animals, he was wide awake, and off for a moonlight adventure.

He padded along the grassy verge of the lane, humming to himself, well content with life. Not far away stretched the broad smooth highway, the great road to London. Motor-cars and lorries whirled along with bright lights illuminating the hedges, spinning like gigantic golden-eyed animals, devouring all before them, and the hedgehog kept away from their roaring speed. They wouldn't follow him down the narrow rough lanes and the tiny green highways, under the arching meadowsweet with its white, sweet flowers dipping to touch his back, and the forests of soft willow-herb. They couldn't hear the rustles among the leaves, or smell the flowers which attracted the white night-moths. He plodded cheerfully on, aware of every movement and smell around him.

He came at last to a gate, and against its bottom bar leaned an old Jack Hare.

"Hello, Jack," said Hedgehog in his friendly way. "How's the world treating you?"

"Pretty middling," replied the hare, taking a straw from his mouth and turning round to the hedgehog. "How's yourself?"

"Oh, pretty fairish," said Hedgehog. "It's a grand night."

" 'Tis indeed! Where might you be going, Hedgehog?"

"Just over the fields to look at the corn a-growing. I allus likes to watch it grow. On a moonlight night it comes on a bit, and there's nothing like a cornfield to my thinking."

"I'll come along with you," said Jack Hare. "I don't mind a bit of adventure. I've seen nobody all day but a couple of magpies, and a few rabbits, and a lost hen. I should like to see the corn a-growing."

"There's a bright lantern hung in the sky to-night," said Hedgehog as they ambled along together, the hare suiting his long steps to the short legs of the hedgehog. "It gives a kind yellow light, that lantern aloft, not trying to the eyes like those twinkly lamps the farm men carry, or those tarrible dazzlers on the motors."

"I can't understand why they bother with those flashing lights when they've got a good lamp in the sky, that costs nothing and is held up for all the world to see," said the hare. "The ways of man are beyond me."

"And me." Hedgehog shook his little head and rattled his prickles in disdain, and very softly under his breath he sang his song.

> *My lantern's the moon,*
> *My candle's a star,*
> *I travel by night,*
> *I wander afar.*

The two crossed a stream, the hare leaping it, the hedgehog paddling in the shallow water, and scrambling on the stones and twigs. By the water's edge, dipping his toes in the dark stream, sat a water-rat.

"How d'ye do?" said Hedgehog. "How's life treating you?"

"Not so bad," replied the water-rat. "Where are you off to? Won't you stay here a while and cool yourselves in my brook? Come and look at the ripples I can make, and the waves all running away from my toes, one chasing another, like swallows in the air."

"We're going over the fields to see the corn a-growing," said Hedgehog, and the hare nodded and echoed: "The green corn a-growing."

"That's a pretty sight, and worth a journey," agreed the water-rat. "It does my heart good to see the corn

a-sprouting and a-springing out of the ground, and waving its head. I'll come too if you don't mind. I've seen nothing all day but a couple of dilly-ducks, and a young frog. I'd like to see something sensible."

They went along together, the hedgehog with his pointed snout and little bright eyes, humming his song, the hare with his great brown eyes glancing to left and right and behind him, and the water-rat with his sleek soft skin and little blunt nose. All the time the moon shone down with a bright silvery light, so that three little dusky shadows ran alongside the three animals.

They made a tiny track in the dewy grass, and they sipped the drops of pearly moisture from the leaves to quench their thirst. They passed a company of cows, lying near the path, and they saw a couple of farm horses cropping close to one another for company. Sweet scents of honeysuckle and briar came to them, and Hedgehog sang his little song once more.

A young hare was racing up and down in the moonlight, and Hedgehog called to him.

"Hello! young Hare," said he. "Why are you in such a hurry?"

The hare sat up, with his long ears twitching as he listened to the little sounds of night.

"I'm a bit mad," said he. "It's the moon. It makes me want to leap when I see that bright light. Can't stop, sorry!" and away he went, galloping over the pasture till he was out of sight.

"Poor fellow! I was just like that once," said Jack Hare, "but I've got a bone in my leg now."

They reached a little knoll, and there they stopped, for in front of them stretched a field of golden wheat. It swayed gently as if an invisible hand stroked it, and even in the silence of the night a murmuring musical sound came from those million million ears of rustling corn.

The moon seemed to stand still in the sky, and look down at the wide cornfield, and the Great Bear blinked his eye and stared.

"Can you hear it muttering?" whispered the hedgehog. "Can you hear the corn talking?"

"Is it alive like us?" asked the little water-rat.

"I can see it breathing, all moving as it takes a big breath," said the hare. "It's a wunnerful sight, a field of corn."

"It's like water," said the water-rat. "It ripples and sighs and murmurs like the water in my brook at home."

The great field with the tall slender stems of wheat growing thick and close, covering fifty acres, seemed to whisper, and the wheat-ears rubbed together as they swayed in the night air, and the sound was that of the sea, a low soft talk of myriad voices.

"This is my adventure," said Hedgehog. "I come here nearly every night, just to see the corn a-growing and a-blowing, and to listen to what it says."

"It's a comforting homely talk," said the hare, "but I can't understand the language. I was never very good at languages. What does it say, Hedgehog?"

"Nay, I c-can't tell you exactly," replied Hedgehog, hesitating, with his head aside, as he listened. "I don't know the words, but they seem to me to be like a song. Listen. Now it's plainer."

He held up his tiny fingered hand, and a myriad rustling voices sang:

> *We are growing, growing, growing,*
> *The corn for the children's bread.*
> *The sap is flowing, flowing, flowing,*
> *From the roots unto the head.*
> *We are the corn,*
> *New-born,*
> *We make the bread.*

The three animals sat breathless, listening to the little sounds and murmurs of the corn's voice. From the woodside came the song of the nightingale, and overhead the moon and stars looked down.

"Aye, that's it!" said Hedgehog. "That's what it tells you. It's growing, ripening, preparing for harvest. It's living, like us."

They turned round and started off home again.

"Good night! Good night!" they said as they parted company. "It was a grand sight. Something to remember. We'll go again, all three of us, when the Harvest moon comes along. Good night."

Hedgehog trundled home to his house-roof under the hedge, and Hare went back to the gate, but the little water-rat sat for a long time on the bank of his stream listening to the murmur of the water, and dreaming of the rustle of the corn.

John Barleycorn

There once lived an old woman who was poor and lonely, for her husband was dead and she had never had any children. She had no one in all the world to care for her except the creatures of the woodland, and these she loved. There was the robin which hopped in at the open door every morning to wish her good-day. She fed him with crumbs and he sang a merry song for her. He flew to the back of her Windsor chair, bobbing up and down as if he were making curtseys to the quality.

"I believe you love me," said she, "or is it cupboard love?"

The robin held his little head on one side, listening to her soft voice, and then he sang again with all his might and main.

In a corner of the garden the old woman kept a few hens. They always ran to welcome her. Even when they were busy scratching the soil and murmuring to each other they rushed off when they saw her bonnet coming down the path among the bushes. She looked at their bright eyes, and she longed for a word from one of them. They laid large white eggs and she never forgot to thank them for their trouble.

"Thank you kindly, my chucky hens," said she, as she gathered up the eggs in her wrinkled hand, and cupped them in her shawl. "Thank you kindly."

"Cluck! Cluck! Cluck!" went the hens, turning their backs and hurrying to eat the scraps she had given them.

"I hope you love me," said she doubtfully. "It may be cupboard love, too, I shouldn't wonder."

Every autumn she went gleaning in the cornfields to gather the ears of corn left by the reapers. Of course she called it "leasing", in the old manner of talk.

She went off at daybreak and stayed in the fields till night, eating her dinner of bread and cheese under the hedge, stooping all day to the stubble. To be out in the warm sunshine, close to the good earth, gathering up the crumbs left from the rich man's table, was a grand life, she thought. She searched among the scarlet pimpernel, and the field pansies growing there in the roots of the wheat and barley. She got so much corn there was a good-sized bag filled to the brim. She picked up the wheat and barley, tasselled and plumed with golden awns, till she had a sheaf. She put it under a tree, bound it with a wisp of straw, and went back for more. At night she stripped the corn from the ears, fanned away the chaff, and sorted the golden grain into a sack.

When gleaning was over, she took the corn to the miller to be ground into flour to make her bread. She kept some grain for her hens. So the gleaning brought her riches and comfort and the farmer always left some extra ears of wheat and barley in the fields for her sake.

One day when the cornfields had been ploughed and prepared for sowing the spring wheat, the old woman went off to the village. She carried a basket of eggs for the market, where she had a seat for selling her wares. She went as usual by the field path which passed through the cornfields. Suddenly she noticed a little green-yellow parcel lying in the middle of the way. It was tied up with

green grasses instead of string. It was exactly the colour
of the fields and she nearly stumbled over it.

She put down her basket of eggs and sat on the low
wall to rest for a while as she examined the packet.

"Whatever can there be inside it?" she asked herself.
"Has a little 'un dropped his dinner packet on the way to
school? But no childer goes this road. I'm about the only
one as ever walks on this forgotten path."

Carefully she untied the knotted grasses, which were
twisted into a fine cord, and fastened in an intricate bow.
It wouldn't do to cut it, even if she had a knife. Careful
folk do not cut string.

She removed the wrapper and saw that it was made of
green leaves stitched together with the tiniest little
stitches to make a cloth.

"Nay, did you ever see the like!" she questioned the
sky and the clouds. She held up the minute cloth in
admiration, and the birds in the trees twittered back to
her in surprise.

She turned again to the parcel. There was another
wrapper, and this one was golden yellow. It was veined
all over like autumn leaves, and it crackled like dry leaves.
It had the sweet smell of the end-of-the-year. This stuff
was stitched with large irregular stitches, and the thread
was brown as earth. She slipped off the yellow string
made of corn stalks, with its tassels of rushes, and held up
the wrappering. It crumbled to pieces under her fingers,
for it was brittle. Underneath was another parcel.

This was wrapped in a cloth of straw, and there was no
string around it. Her old fingers trembled with excitement. She hoped it wasn't a trick played by somebody, a
naughty boy or a fairy man, but it wasn't April Fool's
Day, so who would tease an old poor woman?

She removed the woven straw cover, and inside there

was an egg. It was covered with barley whiskers, and the colour of it was gold.

She was so surprised she cried out in astonishment, "Eh, my goodness! Deary me! Whatever in the world is this?"

She looked around, for she felt in her bones that somebody was watching her. There was nobody to be seen, except the pony in the next field, and a robin hopping along the wall, regarding her with his beady eye. He was as interested as she, but when he saw the egg he flew off to tell his neighbours.

It was not a robin's egg, or thrush's egg, or a plover's egg, or a pheasant's. This gold egg had little pictures painted on it, just as if it were an Easter egg. Perhaps it was an Easter egg, for Easter Sunday was coming in a few weeks, and somebody had sent it in plenty of time. But who had dropped it there?

She turned it over and fumbled for her spectacles, but she hadn't them with her. People don't take their spectacles when they are going to market with eggs to sell. So she peered at the little pictures, and tried to make them out. There was no doubt, one was a growing wheat-ear, another was barley, a third was oats and the fourth was rye.

"A pretty thing and no mistake," she murmured, and again she felt a pair of eyes watching her, and she thought she heard a sound of laughter and a ripple in the ground at her feet.

She wrapped the golden egg in its coverings, and tied it with the string. She lifted her skirts and hid it safely away in her pocket, deep among her many petticoats. Then she picked up her market-basket, and went on to the village.

She sold her eggs very quickly that day, and with the money she bought some sausages, and tea and sugar, and a piece of red flannel for a cloak-lining. Her fingers patted her pocket where the golden egg lay, but she was too shy to show it to the man who sold cups and mugs at the next stall, or to the woman who had black puddings and chitterlings on the other side. They might have cracked the frail shell, or laughed at her tale.

When she got home it was dusk, but no light shone from the cottage to welcome her. Only the robin sang his good-night song in the apple-tree as she looked under the shell in her rockery for the house-key.

"Aye, my dear Bobby," she called. "Do you know what thing I've found? Had ye summut to do wi' it?"

The robin shook his little head and flew off.

She unlocked her door and poked up the kitchen fire, and threw a handful of sticks on it, so that a blaze shot out and a pleasant glow shone on the dresser with its row of jugs and plates. She cooked the sausages and made the tea. The golden egg lay on the dresser-end, and she kept stopping to touch it, and to peep at it, and to hold it in her hands.

"A double-yoked goose egg, maybe," said she to herself. "But I daresn't crack it, for the shell's so pretty. It would be a sin and a shame to spoil it."

Whether it was the heat of the branches blazing in the hearth, or the warmth of the old woman's fingers that continually caressed it, I do not know, but something moved within the egg. The shell went Crick-cr-cr-crack! Crack! It fell apart, and a little face grinned up at her.

"Mercy me! Whatever's this?" she cried aloud.

A voice as shrill as a cricket's and as sweet as a wren's piped back to her.

"John Barleycorn. John Barleycorn," it said, but the words were uttered with such shrill intensity they sounded like utter gibberish to the old woman.

A tiny child lay there, nestling in the broken egg-shell, stretching its legs, which had been cramped in the egg, holding out its skinny arms to the firelight, smiling with a crinkled little smile on its small pointed face.

She brought the candle near, and fetched her spectacles to look at the child. She wasn't quite sure whether he was a bird of some kind, for on his head grew fluffy yellow feathers instead of hair, and he seemed to have a pair of wings on his back. His eyes were blue as the speedwell, that little bird's-eye flower that covers the banks in spring, and his mouth was curved in a cupid's bow. He was a beautiful little boy, or perhaps a fairy child. She couldn't make him out at all. One doesn't find a baby in an egg-shell every day of the week.

She put her old puckered hand under him, and gingerly carried him to the fire. How he kicked and laughed! A thrill of joy ran through her as she felt his warm flesh and his tiny pulsing heart beating on her hand. They weren't wings either, and she was glad of that, for, when she looked more closely, she saw they were gold hairs as thick as the awns of barley, and they dropped off in her

hands. She was pleased he hadn't got wings and couldn't fly away. His tiny ears were pointed, silky, and hairy, but that didn't matter. He was a darling little creature, whatever he was, and she loved him.

"Oh, the tiny wee bairn," she cried, laughing at his funny little face, and she gave him a spoonful of milk.

"Here, sup this up," said she. "It'll warm ye."

He drank greedily, and opened his mouth for more and more. Already he seemed to be growing. His little arms lost their wrinkles, his face became smooth and sweet to look upon.

She cut off a morsel of her red flannel and made him a cloak, and she wrapped him up like a little doll to keep him warm.

She made a bed in the pie-dish, and lined it with sheep's wool, from her store of pickings from the hedges. There she laid him while she heated up her sausages and drank her cold tea. It wasn't long before he struggled to his feet and climbed over the edge of the dish. He carried the red flannel on his shoulders like a lady's train, and walked across the table. He peeped into the glass salt-cellar, and tasted the salt. He liked that, and he nibbled the hard grains. Then he found the sugar basin, and there he sat, licking his fingers as he dipped them in the bowl.

"You funny little boy," said the old woman. "What shall I call you? Thumbkin? Fingertip? Bittikins?"

"John Barleycorn," said the child, and now his voice was so clear the old woman was quite startled.

"So you can speak, you wee thing. John Barleycorn, is it? I'll take ye to church soon to be christened by the parson, all good and proper, John Barleycorn."

The little creature yawned, stretched his arms, and suddenly fell fast asleep on the tablecloth among the spoons. She lifted him up, and spoke tenderly to him as she placed him in the pie-dish bed for the night. Then, when she had sewn a little red coat and a nightgown from the flannel and fashioned a small vest of wool she went to her own bed in the corner of the room.

Never had she spent such an exciting day in all her long life, she thought, as she lay watching the darting shadows on the wall, and the flickering firelight which glanced on the tiny figure in the dish. The light made his skin glow like molten gold; his feathery hair shone like rubies. He tossed in his sleep and stretched his arms to the shadows that seemed to be hovering around him, bending to watch him.

Once, when the old woman had been fast asleep, she awoke suddenly, thinking there was somebody in the room. The tiny boy slept there, but a field of tall ripe corn was growing around him, higher than the table, waving like a fire, and the sound of the rustling ears made strange music. She was frightened, as she watched the corn sway to and fro.

Then a lady of wonderful beauty rose from the stalks. A benign face leaned over the child, and golden fingers touched his cheeks. The corn was swept up in her arms and she faded away.

The room was bright with firelight. It must have been a dream. The flashes of fire from a fallen log had made the effect of golden corn filling the room. Yes, it must have been a dream, but she thought of tales she had heard in her childhood of a corn goddess who looked after the harvests throughout the land. She hoped the little boy would still be there at day-break.

He awoke before she did and lay kicking his legs, laughing and singing a wild little song like a bird's.

"You sing as bonny as the sky-lark," she cried, smiling at his antics. She blew up the fire while he sprang to his feet and watched her with intent gaze. He puffed out his little cheeks and blew too, and didn't the fire go well that morning! It was the same all through the day. He imitated everything she did, and kept her laughing like a young girl. Her years seemed to fall away from her with such a merry elf in the house.

"I must take you to church to be baptized," she told him. "I must have a christened child. You may be pagan, or summut."

How he laughed at her! He said the words after her, speaking in a tiny clear voice which did her heart good to hear.

"White for Christians," said she. "I mun make ye a white robe, though I doubt if you're the kind to wear a christening robe. Coat and trousers for you, I think. You can't wear that red flannel coat at your christening, can you?"

She hunted in an old leather trunk and brought out a piece of white embroidered lawn, which had been her wedding veil. She cut it into a christening gown for him. It took all day to make it, but she was a neat seamstress, for she had been a lady's maid in her youth.

"It's like making a dress for a dolly," said she.

"A Corn dolly," said he. "John Barleycorn and a Corn dolly."

"Nay, don't chatter so much," she admonished him, wagging her finger at him. "If ye talks as much as this at one day old, how much will ye talk at a year old?"

He grabbed her brass thimble and stuck it on his head. Then he pranced up and down the table, like a little king wearing a crown. He was up to tricks all that livelong day, but at night he slept soundly in the pie-dish, as good as a human child.

c

Again came the waving corn, and the old woman awoke to see the radiant vision leaning over him, touching his golden cheek. The beauty faded, the corn sank into the earth, and only the flashing firelight remained to gild the tiny figure lying there.

The next day the old woman carried him to the rectory. The good rector was much astonished, you may be sure, to see such a wee fellow in a market basket. However, he was a countryman himself, so he didn't ask too many questions.

"What name do you wish this child to have?" he asked.

"John Barleycorn," said the old woman. "You see, sir, I found him, at least I kind of found him, in Farmer Taylor's barleyfield, where I goes a-leasing. It's a good field, and I've got many a peck of barleycorns from it, so if you don't mind, sir, I would like John Barleycorn to be his name."

"Well," hummed the rector. "It's a queer name, an outlandish name. Why not call him Moses? He was found out of doors, and although he wasn't in the bulrushes, he was in the barleyfield, not far from the pond."

"Moses. Yes. That's nice," said the old woman.

"Then you could give him your own surname of Winkle. Moses Winkle. How do you like that?"

The old woman liked it very much, for she was partial to Bible names, and it would be very nice, she thought, to have a child called Winkle after her. So she nodded her head in agreement. She didn't notice the little fellow, shaking his yellow feathery curls, frowning with all his wee might.

They entered the ancient church, and at once all the stone faces on the walls looked down and began to smile when they saw who was in the basket. The tiny child smiled back at bishop and king and queer wide-mouthed men carved on those old walls. His quick eyes darted round as he lay in the old woman's arms, up to the arching roof with its king-posts, away to the altar. He was carried to the beautiful old font, to be baptized where generations of children had been christened since Norman days, but in all the centuries never a baby like this had been dipped in holy water.

There was a stir among the tall wooden angels carved under the great roof, and a flutter of their outspread wings. There was a movement among all the queer grimacing stone faces on the chancel arches, and sleepy eyes goggled and mouths opened and shut.

"John Barleycorn! John Barleycorn!" The whisper seemed to go round the walls, circling high in the timbered roof, echoing to the tower, floating to the bells.

"Where are the godparents?" asked the rector, looking about for the village people who should have been present.

From out of the shadows of the church came two majestic figures, moving serenely, gliding down the aisle with a rustle like the wind in the corn. One was a fair-haired man, tall and golden-skinned like a god. His strong arms were bare and he carried a sickle of shining light. The other was a woman, young and beautiful, draped in a green shawl, carrying a sheaf of ripe corn in her arms as if she had just returned from gleaning.

They took the baby without speaking, but the old woman was so surprised she stood open-mouthed, for she recognized the godmother as the one who leaned over the tiny child in the field of growing corn during the night-time.

When the rector asked the child's name the words "John Barleycorn, John Barleycorn" came ringing out like bells. Everything in the church answered, every angel

and carved figure spoke. There was no question of Moses
Winkle, and John Barleycorn was the name given to the
baby. The godparents turned to the old woman standing
so meekly there. One dropped a little gold spoon in her
wrinkled hand, and its shape was a wheat-ear. The other
gave her a little gold bowl with barley ears engraved upon
its side, and John Barleycorn's name upon it.

Then they walked away out of the church door, into
the sunshine. When the startled rector hurried after them
to the door, they had vanished, and nobody saw them any
more.

Now John Barleycorn grew very fast, and in a few
months he was full-grown. He stood tall and slim and
straight as an arrow, about three feet high. His feathery
hair was like a gold mop that waved on his head in the
wind. His feet were long and narrow, and he ran very
swiftly. His hands were beautiful and his fingers could
make anything he set about. He could weave baskets from
osiers and rushes, so delicate and well-made that the
people at the market bought every one. He could cut
musical pipes from elder and ash, and produce such sweet
tunes from them that even the birds stopped singing to
listen to him. He carved little people from pieces of wood,
but they were strange queer men he made, such as live
underground, and the old woman put them out of sight.
Sometimes he carved wheat-ears and barley-ears so
exquisitely, they would rustle as he held them up in the
wind, and these the old woman sold to the shops. To
amuse himself he took a burnt stick from the fire and with
the charcoal he drew flowers and birds and animals with
startling exactness. All these were his games, his pleasures.
He worked hard too.

The garden flourished in an astonishing manner when
he planted roots or scattered seeds.

The fruit trees were laden with apples and plums, although he only touched the branches and spoke to the buds, or leaned his golden cheek against the trunks. It was as if everything loved John Barleycorn, and he loved everything in return.

He went with the old woman to market, and carried a small basket of eggs while she carried the large basket in which he had been taken to his christening. At first people stopped to stare at his bright gold hair, which they said was the colour of corn, but they soon got used to him. He held their horses for a penny and he ran their errands. He was willing to work for all.

Sometimes he went alone to the church, and gazed up at the stone figures and the wooden angels under the roof. The gargoyles and saints seemed to delight in his company, and they blinked their eyes, and screwed up their mouths and spoke in muffled voices.

"John Barleycorn. We remember you, John Barleycorn, our friend. Long ago we played with you, John Barleycorn."

Then he ran out to the churchyard and danced among the tombstones, and planted flowers on the graves.

"Thank you, John Barleycorn. Thank you. We remember you, John Barleycorn," whispered the voices of the dead.

His greatest joy was to go into the cornfield, to walk along the verges, and seek for the small flowers that grew there, to laugh at the hares and tease the hedgehogs and scare the cock pheasant from trampling the corn. He came home decked with garlands of cornflowers, and purple corncockle, and scarlet poppies.

"I can see where you've been, John," said his mother, for the old woman thought of the child as her very own bairn. "You've been to watch the barley growing. You shall come with me a-leasing when the corn's cut."

"I want to earn my living, Mother," said he one day.
"I want to help at the farm for harvest."

"Nay, you are too little, my wee son," she replied.
"Wait till you grow bigger."

"I'm grown up, Mother. I'm as tall as the corn now,"
he pouted. "I'm full-grown."

"You would get lost in the great field, lost in the forest
of barley stalks," said she. "You would be cut by the
reapers."

However, when the men began to reap the harvest,
little John Barleycorn went to the farmer and got the

job of making the shocks of corn. They were as big as himself, and the men laughed to see him, but they were filled with admiration for the way the small boy worked. There was a magic in his touch, for with little trouble he shocked the corn and kept pace with the harvesters. Sometimes it was difficult to distinguish the boy from the barley sheaves, they were the same height, and the same golden colour, and they seemed to move together, corn swaying to boy, and boy binding the sheaves and caressing them as if he loved them.

At the Harvest Home the farmer put little John Barleycorn on the last wagon, on the great load of sheaves. The white horses drew the load, and there sat little John Barleycorn, wreathed in scarlet poppies and blue cornflowers and honeysuckle, like a king of the cornfield.

On the cart was the harvest doll, called the Kern Baby, which the oldest worker had made from some good ears of corn.

She was the symbol of good luck to the harvest. Little John Barleycorn sat by her side, his golden hair like the barley blowing in the wind, his face smiling, his blue eyes the colour of the cornflowers.

The harvest men sang a song as the great swaying wain laden with corn went through the fields to the rick yard and barns.

> *We have ploughed, we have sowed,*
> *We have reaped, and we have mowed.*
> *We have brought home every load.*
> *Hip! Hip! Hip! Harvest Home!*

They had the harvest supper in the farmyard and John Barleycorn danced on the table among the tankards of ale and the boiled beef and suet dumpling.

"It's been a bumper crop this year," said the farmer, "and I do believe it's all along of John Barleycorn here. I shall send your mother a sack of corn in payment, John, for she's getting old to go a-leasing."

"Thank you, sir," said little John. "She can't stoop very well, but can I go, sir? I want to go a-leasing. I've been looking forward to it all my life."

"All your short life," laughed the farmer. "All right."

So little John Barleycorn went a-leasing by himself, and the old woman insisted on coming to the gate of the cornfield with him, and bringing his dinner and tea in a basin with a cloth over it.

She could see the small figure walking the fields, stooping close to the earth, and talking to somebody who was invisible. He was laughing and nodding, and now and then he took someone's hand in his. Then he gathered up the scattered corn, and clasped it to him. He gathered as much in a day as his mother had done in a week. He seemed to have grown older in that one day leasing, alone with the cornfield.

At the Harvest Festival he went to church with his mother. A tiny little person, his head scarcely reached the top of the pew, and he was put on a hassock. All went well, till the harvest hymn was sung. Then John Barleycorn piped up in such a shrill treble that the sound of it rang through the church and startled the congregation. They looked round to see who was warbling so loudly. They gazed up and about them, for somebody else was singing too. Every carved face on the old church walls, every wooden angel with outstretched wings on that grand roof, every beam and stone in the ancient building gave thanks to God Almighty for the splendid harvest. Never was such singing heard in a church!

The hymn came to an end, the organ tones died away, the voices were quiet and there was an astonished silence. Then there was a scamper of little boots and little John Barleycorn ran down the nave to the chancel, where he sat among the sheaves of corn and the miniature thatched rick and the long loaf of bread brought in from the farm for the festival.

The rector hesitated a moment, and the little choir-boys gasped, and the churchwarden stepped forward. Something restrained them all, and the service went on. Little John Barleycorn looked like a cherub as he sat there with one arm around a sheaf of corn, his gold hair sweeping into the barley, his cheek resting against it. His golden skin was exactly the same colour as the ripe corn. He *was* the corn and nobody could turn him away.

"Eh, John. You shouldn't have done it," said his mother afterwards as they walked home. "I couldn't believe my own eyes. It's not proper. Eh, I was shocked."

"But, Mother, I was thanking God. I had to go there. I had to be with the barley sheaves. They are my brothers, Mother."

When the corn ricks were thatched, and the thatcher made the little crown of corn to decorate the top of the rick, John Barleycorn watched him. The labourer tied some ears together in a tassel, and twisted a straw band round it, to form a crown, with the ears poking through the little archway of straw. John Barleycorn followed him up the ladder with it, and there he stayed, night and day, only coming down now and then to visit his mother.

He disappeared after that, but each spring when the barley came up in the fields, little John Barleycorn came to stay with his foster mother, to help the corn to grow, and to be the guest of honour at the Harvest Home.

They all sang around him the harvest song:

We have ploughed, we have sowed,
We have reaped, and we have mowed.
We have brought home every load.
Hip! Hip! Hip! Harvest Home!

And as long as John Barleycorn came to the fields the corn grew tall and strong and the ears were large and well filled.

Country Mice meet Church Mouse

Jemima and Jeremy were two little field-mice who lived in a house under the hawthorn tree on the common, and they had a strange adventure one fine autumn day. It was a morning of sunshine, and golden light filled the fields of ripened corn, and scarlet poppies grew in the hedgerows.

The little mice ran along the edge of the big cornfield, through the tall stalks of the wheat, on a tiny track invisible to the eyes of people, but clear to the bright eyes of the mice. The track led to the village, but it seemed a long way to the mice. The harvest mouse peeped from the doorway of her round house high in the cornstalks, and the mice stopped for a talk.

"Please, Mrs Harvest, are we on the right path to the village?" asked Jeremy Mouse.

"Yes, my children," said the comfortable harvest mouse. "Go straight on, and under the gate, and turn to your right."

"Thank you, Mrs Harvest Mouse," replied Jeremy politely, and he took Jemima's hand and led her through the forest of cornstalks to the gate and the village green.

Children were running about, and there was an excitement in the air. So the two mice hurried under a small gate which had a wooden roof over it, into a large garden,

with upright stones. They thought it was a garden, for there
were many flowers lying in the grass, garlands of flowers,
but it was a churchyard, with old graves and crosses.

The two ran lightly over a gravestone, where some
flowers lay, but a dark head appeared near them and Mr
Mole stood there, waiting.

He shook his fist at the two strangers, who leapt down
and bowed to him.

"Go away," said he sternly. "This is not a place for
field-mice, not for bad little mice like you. This is the
quiet garden for good mice who always behave themselves."

"We are good mice, sir," said Jeremy quickly. He
danced back on the gravestone and wiped a dark stain
from the stone with a dock-leaf. "We are very good mice.
We won't harm anything, sir," said he to the mole.

Jemima stroked a butterfly which settled near her and
the butterfly waved its wings up and down with pleasure
at her soft touch. Jeremy waved his paw to a jackdaw who
sat listening, and he let a ladybird settle on his fur. "My
mother says we are good," said Jeremy. "Do let us stay.
We like this garden and no children are playing here. It is
safe and quiet."

"It is Sunday," said the mole sternly. "People are
coming to church. Go away. You are not wanted."

The mole dug a hole near the grave, and disappeared.

"Where has he gone?" asked Jemima.

"He's looking for bones," jeered the jackdaw. "Bones
like yours," he added, and he flew off with a cackle.

The church door was open and there was a trail of
leaves and berries and broken stalks of flowers, with here
and there a poppy and a rose head. Jeremy and Jemima
Mouse entered the porch, and leapt down a step into the
great empty church.

There were flowers everywhere, for it was the Harvest Festival and the decorators had finished their work. "How pretty it is," whispered Jemima, looking round at the chrysanthemums on the font, and the dahlias decorating a little wooden house which had a flight of wooden stairs. "A house of flowers!"

Jeremy ran up the stairs to the pulpit and gazed over the edge at the church below. There was a big sheaf of corn on the ledge and he ate some ears of wheat and tossed a few down to Jemima below.

"What a nice little house," said he, "I could go to sleep here," and he ran back to his sister. She had found a long loaf of crusty bread, freshly baked, resting against a stone figure of a sleeping man. She nibbled a little and found it very good. Then she climbed up to look at the statue. The stone man's feet rested on the back of a little dog, and the dog seemed to lick its lips when it saw Jemima perched there. "Poor little dog," said Jemima. She ate more of the wheat-ears which hung in tassels from each wooden pew. There was a sweet smell everywhere, and plenty of food for a hundred mice.

"This is like a storehouse of food," said Jeremy, as he nibbled some red berries and swung on the cornstalks. They bit the edges of a prayer-book and tasted the wool of an embroidered kneeler. They skated on a brass tablet let into the floor and admired their own faces reflected there.

"It could be brighter," said Jemima. "Let us polish it."

She took out her tiny leafy handkerchief and rubbed the brass, and Jeremy removed his scarf and polished too. Soon the brass was bright as gold, and the words on it shone as never before. They were so busy that they did not notice someone was watching them.

"What are you doing here?" asked a cross voice, with a squeak in it. "What do you think you are doing in our church, you bold little field-mice?"

A black mouse, thin and tall, in a black coat and black leather boots, came down the aisle and stood over them.

"Why do you come to our church, to bring your untidy ways? Why do you come here and eat our feast, that we have only once a year, when there are many poor thin church mice waiting to come and feast?"

"Please, sir, please, sir, we are very sorry, sir. We didn't know," stammered Jemima. "We saw the door open and here are the grains of corn from our cornfields, where we live."

"This is our special day," growled the church mouse. "No food on ordinary days, no wheat-sheaves, or loaves of bread. We starve and we have to nibble the hymn-books and hassocks, the floor polish and the fringes on the cloths, and the crumbs the choirboys drop for us," said the old weary church mouse.

Jemima felt so sorry that tears came into her eyes.

"You have polished that brass plate very well," said the church mouse, relenting as he saw her sorrow. "If you polish the candlesticks over yonder, the Vicar will be pleased."

"Yes, sir," said Jeremy and Jemima, and they pattered quickly down the aisle to the chancel and ran up the big brass candlesticks to polish them.

They were busily working on these when the church bells rang out a merry peal, and the doors were opened wide. Into the church came people, all smiling with happiness to see the flowers and wheat sheaves. Jeremy

and Jemima polished as quickly as they could, scurrying up and down, and nobody saw them. Now and then they took a nibble of the wax candle, but a man came across to light the candles and the two mice ran swiftly to the ground and hid in corners.

Down in the chancel they saw a tiny black flag waving on the church floor, a little black wing which fluttered piteously, and they heard a faint squeak. "Help! Help! Help!" was the cry.

Jemima went to look and she saw a baby bat which had hurt its wing and could not fly.

Quickly she climbed into a dark corner behind the altar and gathered up a thick spider's web which hung to the wall.

"Excuse me, Mrs Spider," said she to a large angry spider which came forward to stop her. "Excuse me, but a spider's web is the best cure for a torn wing or a cut leg," said she.

"It is the ancient cure," agreed the spider, "but nobody bothers nowadays. Who is hurt? Not a choirboy, surely? They have no wings." She laughed hoarsely.

"No, a little bitbat," said Jemima, and she hurried across the floor with the web. She laid it over the cut wing and bound a piece of web to keep the wing in shape. Then she lifted up the little creature and placed it on a flower petal. It fluttered its wing slowly, waveringly, it rose in the air, sailed across the church and up into the oak beams where its mother was anxiously watching.

"That was a good little mouse," said the bat as she embraced her child.

A choirboy had seen Jemima and he threw a hymn-book at her, but she only smiled and sat down on it.

The boys began to sing. The organ poured out rich music and all the people stood and joined in. Jemima also stood and sang and her little voice squeaked an octave above the voices of the choir, so that it made a harmonious cadence.

> *All things bright and beautiful,*
> *All creatures great and small,*
> *All things wise and wonderful,*
> *The Lord God made them all*

sang the people, and Jemima crept near Jeremy and said, "We are creatures small, aren't we Jeremy?"

"Yes, very small, but they know about us," whispered Jeremy.

The choirboy was watching them and the mice felt nervous. Quietly they stepped down the chancel and walked one behind the other down the aisle. People's eyes were on the flowers, on the lights and on the stained glass windows. They did not notice two little strangers who moved quietly like two small shadows, but the church mouse watched them go.

"Goodbye, my cousins," he squeaked. "Goodbye. You are good little creatures after all."

The bats in the belfry flew out over the roof of the church, singing with the people. "All creatures great and small," they squeaked.

Jeremy and Jemima crept through a hole in the door and went out to the graveyard and to the bright sun.

"Safe," murmured Jeremy. "I thought that boy would try to catch us."

"We are creatures small," said Jemima. "They said so. Let's go home and tell our mother."

So off they went, back through the cornfield, under the nest of the sleeping harvest mouse, among the butterflies and beetles, the frogs and the field-mice, the hedgehogs and the spiders, all the way home to their mother.

"Welcome in, my dears," said Mrs Mouse. "Where have you been? I've been listening to the church bells. It must be a special day, for they rang so loudly."

"We've been to Church, Mother, and it was nice," said Jemima, hugging her mother.

"And it was all full of flowers and food, so we had our dinner there," added Jeremy.

"And we are all creatures great and small," said Jemima.

"Are you, my dears?" asked Mrs Mouse.

"The Lord God made us all," added Jeremy. "They said so, all singing with choirboys."

"It must be true," said Mrs Mouse, and she smiled in happiness.

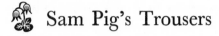 Sam Pig's Trousers

Sam Pig was always hard on his trousers. He tore them on the brambles and hooked them in the gorse bushes. He lost little pieces of them in the hawthorns, and he left shreds among the spiky thistles. He rubbed them thread-bare with sliding down the rocks of the high pastures, and he wore them into holes when he scrambled through hedges. One always knew where Sam Pig had been by the fragments of check trousers which clung to thorn and crooked twig. The birds were very glad, and they took bits to make their nests. The rooks had little snippets like gay pennons dangling from their rookery in the elms, and the chaffinches and yellow-hammers mixed the thread with sheep's wool to line their beds. It seemed as if Sam Pig would provide material for everybody's home in the trees and hedgerows, but trousers won't last for ever, and Sam's were nearly done.

Sister Ann patched the seats and put pieces into the front. She stitched panels in the two sides, and then she patched and repatched the patches until there was none of the original trousers left. They were a conglomeration of stripes and plaids and spotted scraps, all herring-boned and cross-stitched with green thread.

"Sam's trousers are like a patchwork quilt," remarked Tom, when Ann held up the queer little garments one evening after she had mended them.

"Pied and speckled like a magpie," said Bill.

Sam Pig leaned out of the truckle bed where he lay wrapped in a blanket, waiting for Ann to finish the mending. They were the only trousers the little pig possessed, and he had to go to bed early on mending nights.

"I like them patched," said he indignantly. "Don't mock at them. I love my old trousers and their nice patches. It's always a surprise when Ann finishes them. Look now! There's a green patch on top of a black patch, on top of a yellow patch, on top of a blue one. And there's lots of pockets hidden among the patches, spaces where I can keep things. When Ann's stitches burst I stuff things in between."

"Yes," frowned Ann. "I've already taken out a lady-bird, and a piece of honeycomb, and some bees and a frog that was leaping up and down, and a stag-beetle that was fighting, not to mention sundry pebbles and oak-apples and snail shells! No wonder you look a clumsy shape with all those things hidden in your patches, Sam! All corners and lumps, you are!"

Sam curled himself under the blanket and laughed till he made the bed shake. She hadn't found the most important thing of all, something that was hidden under the largest patch! If she did——!

Just then Ann gave a shrill cry and dropped the trousers.

"Oh! They've bitten me! Your trousers bit my finger!" she exclaimed, and she put her hand in her mouth and sucked it.

"Trousers can't bite," said Tom, but Sam dived deeper under the blanket, and laughed all the more.

"What is it, Sam?" asked Tom sternly. "Confess! What is hidden there in your trousers?"

There was no answer, but from the patch came a pair of ears and two bright eyes. A white mouse poked out its little head. It stared at Ann, it peeped at Sam, and then it bolted down the table leg and into a hole in the floor.

"Now you've lost her! You've lost Jemima!" said Sam crossly, coming up from the blankets. "She was my pet mouse, and you've lost her. She was a most endearing creature. I kept her in that patch and fed her on crumbs. Is her family safe?"

"Family?" cried Ann, shrilly.

"Family?" echoed Bill and Tom.

"Yes. She has four children. They all live in the patch. They have a nest there. I helped Jemima to make it. I'm the godfather to the children. They know me very well."

Ann hurriedly unpicked the stitches and brought out a small round nest with four pink mice inside it.

"There they are! Aren't they charming creatures?" cried Sam. "But they will be lonely without their mother. You must put them by the hole in the floor, Ann, and Jemima will come for them. She'll miss her warm home in my trousers, and the food I gave her."

Ann carried the nest and placed it close to the hole. In a minute the mother appeared and enticed her brood away.

"Good-bye, Sam," she squealed in a shrill voice, thin as a grasshopper's chirp. "Good-bye, Sam, and thank you for your hospitality. We are going to travel. It is time my children saw something of the world."

"Good-bye," called Sam, leaning out of bed. "I shall miss you terribly, but we may meet again some day. The world is small."

"Hm!" sniffed Ann Pig. "The world may be small, but surely there is room in it for a family of white mice without their coming to live in a patch in your trousers, Sam."

She threaded her needle and took up a bodkin and cleared away all the odds and ends the mice had left, their pots and frying-pan and toasting fork. She tossed the bits of cheese in the fire and frowned as she brought out bacon rind.

"Bacon in the house of the four pigs is an insult," said she sternly.

"It came from the grocer's shop, Ann. Really it did! Jemima's husband brought it for the family," protested Sam.

"Then it's quite time you had a new pair of trousers Sam. Jemima's husband bringing bacon rinds! I won't have it! These mice are the last straw!" cried Ann, and she banged the trousers and shook them and threw them back to Sam.

"Yes," agreed Bill. "It is time you had new breeks. We can't have a menagerie in our house. You'll keep ants and antelopes hidden in your patches, Sam, if you go on like this."

"Bears and bisons," said Tom, shaking his head at Sam.

"Crocodiles and cassowaries," whispered Sam, quivering with laughter.

"It's no laughing matter. Trousers don't grow on gooseberry bushes."

"I don't want a new pair," pouted Sam. "I know this pair, and they are very comfortable. I know every stitch and cranny, and every ridge and crease and crumple," He pulled the trousers on and shook himself.

"These will soon be quite worn out. One more tear and they will be done," said Ann. "We must get another pair, and where the stuff is to come from in these hard times I don't know. You'd better go collecting, all of you."

"Collecting what? Trousers? From the scarecrows?" asked Sam.

"No. Sheep's wool. Get it off the hedges and bushes and fences. Everywhere you go you must gather the wool left by the sheep when they scramble through gaps and rub their backs on posts. Then I'll dye the wool and spin it, and make a new pair for you."

Each day the pigs gathered sheep's wool. They picked it off the wild-rose trees, where it was twisted among the thorns. They got it from low fences under which the sheep had squeezed, and from the rough trunks of hawthorns and oaks where they had rubbed their backs. Sam found a fine bunch of fleecy wool where the flock had pushed under the crooked boughs of an ancient tree to sleep in the hollow beneath. It was surprising what a quantity of wool there was lying about in the country lanes, and each day they brought back their small sacks filled to the brim.

Ann washed the little fleeces and hung them up to dry. The wool was white as snow when she had finished dipping it in the stream. She tied it to a stout stick and swung it in the sunshine till it was dry and light as a feather.

Bill filled a bowl with lichens and mosses and pieces of bark, and Ann dyed the wool.

"What colour will it be?" asked Sam, anxiously peering at it. "I don't want brown or grey or anything dull."

"It looks like drab," confessed Ann.

"Oh dear! What a dingy shade!" sighed Sam. "I don't want miserable gloomy trousers, or I shall be a gloomy little pig."

"I'm afraid they *are* going to be sad trousers, Sam," said Ann, stirring them with a stick. "I'm sorry, but this is the colour, and there's one good thing, it is the colour of dirt."

"Gloomy and black as a pitchy night in winter," said Sam.

So off he went to the woods. He picked some crimson bryony berries, and scarlet rose-hips, and bright red toadstools. He brought them back and dropped them into the dye.

"Ann! Ann! Come and look," he called, and he held up the fleece on the end of the stirring stick.

"Oh Sam! Bright red! A glorious colour," cried Ann.

"Like a sunset," exclaimed Tom, admiringly.

"Like a house on fire," said Bill.

Out rushed Sam again, for blueberries and blue geranium and borage. He dipped another wisp of sheep's wool into the juices and brought it out blue as a wood in bluebell time.

They dried the wool, and Ann fastened it to her little spinning-wheel. She spun a length of red yarn and then a length of blue. Then she knitted a new pair of trousers, in blue and red checks, bright and bold, with plenty of real pockets.

When Sam Pig walked out in his new trousers all the animals and birds came to admire him. Even the Fox stopped to stare at Sam.

"As red as my brush," he murmured, and the Hedgehog said, "As pretty a pair of trousers as ever I seed in all my prickly life."

When Sam met the white mouse and her family they refused to visit his new pockets.

"We like something quieter," whispered the mouse. "You are too dazzling for us nowadays, Sam. Besides, we have found a lodging in an old boot. It suits us better."

"As you will, Jemima," shrugged Sam. He sauntered off to show himself to acquaintances in the fields, to visit his old haunts in wood and lane.

Soon his trousers lost their brightness, as they took on the hues of the woodland. They were striped green from the beech trunks, smeared with the juices of blackberry and spindle, parched by the brown earth herself. The sun faded them, the rain shrunk them, and the colours were softened by the moist airs.

"I declare! There is no difference in Sam's trousers," Ann remarked one day. "These might be the old check trousers; they are marked and stained in just the same way. I haven't patched them yet, but I can see a hole."

"Yes," said Sam, slyly, and he brought a dormouse from his pocket. "Here is a little friend who lives with me, and he's waiting for a patch to make his winter sleeping-quarters, Ann."

"Get along with you," cried Ann, and she chased him out with a besom. But her eyes were twinkling as she watched her young brother dance down the garden path with his dormouse perched on his arm.

The white mouse Jemima in this story is of course not the same character as the field-mouse Jemima in *Country Mice meet Church Mouse*.

The Wind in a Frolic

One day the Wind awoke from a little nap under the
quiet trees. He stretched himself lazily, and yawned with
wide-open mouth, so that the bees and butterflies resting
on the flowers were blown away by the tiny gust.

"Oh! Ho-o-o!" he yawned, again. "I'll go for a stroll,
and say how-do-ye-do to the village folk. I'm sure they've
missed me lately. I'll go and cheer them up, play with
them, amuse them. Yes, that's what I'll do to-day."

He picked up his long length from the mossy ground,
and stalked off down the path, snapping twigs from the
trees with his slender fingers, blowing the leaves with his
breath.

Now he hadn't gone far when he met a little boy going
to school. Such a neat little, nice little, clean little boy,
with his cap on his head, and his school-bag on his back!

"How d'ye do?" said the Wind, and he put out one
thin finger, twitched the cap and flung it up in a sycamore-
tree. There it hung till the nice little boy climbed up and
got it down, but his hands were dirty, and his hair was
awry. The Wind sat on the ground watching, waiting for
the little boy to laugh.

"Bother the wind!" exclaimed the little boy, and he
stuffed his cap in his pocket and went whistling to school.

"That was clever of me," said the Wind, "but he
wasn't amused. I must do something better next time."

He went a bit farther, and overtook a little girl. A few drops of rain were falling by this time, and she put up her umbrella.

"I always think umbrellas are such comical things," said the Wind, "don't you?" The little girl answered never a word, but held tight to the handle when she felt the Wind's presence.

"Away it goes!" cried the Wind, putting his face under it, and giving a small puff. Away it went, inside out, and the Wind laughed and laughed at the funny sight. But the little girl didn't laugh. She ran after her umbrella, and picked it up sadly. It was her birthday umbrella the Wind had spoilt, but of course the Wind didn't know that.

"Dear-a-me," said the Wind. "I thought that was amusing. I must find some one else to tease."

He went rollicking along the road, and the cows and horses turned their backs or stood close to the hedges for shelter. Then he saw a farm man carrying a load of hay on his back. The Wind blew and blew, till the man staggered against a wall and the hay went floating off in the air.

The Wind laughed to see the sight, but the man grumbled and groaned as he collected it together again, and tied it with a rope.

"The wind's something awful!" said he crossly, and the Wind, very much surprised, skipped away to find someone with a sense of humour.

Along came a woman with a basket of eggs, and the Wind hurried up to her.

"Madam," said he politely, taking off his pointed hat. "Madam, may I carry your basket for you?" He put a hand on the basket, but the woman felt the strong gale around her, and held on with all her might. What was

happening to the weather, for the wind to blow like that
all of a sudden? she wondered. Her skirts flew out behind
her, her hat blew off, but she wouldn't let the basket go.

Then the Wind tossed an egg in the air, and it fell with
a splash of yellow.

"Isn't that a joke! Ha! Ha! If only you would give me your basket, I would show you even funnier things. Eggs sailing in the air, and dropping like raindrops!"

"Goodness!" cried the woman. "There's one of my eggs! Twopence gone. This wind's a regular nuisance." She held the basket close to her side to protect it, but the Wind had flown away to find someone else.

He blew the hens in the farmyard, so that they ran squawking to the barn, and he drove the dog to the kennel. He shook the sign outside the village inn, and rattled the shutters on the wall. He threw a slate off the roof, and dropped a chimney-pot. The Wind chuckled at all these pranks, but the people frowned and shut their doors.

Then away went the Wind, away, away, over the fields and woods. He felt very unhappy, for nobody laughed, nobody wanted the Wind's frolic. He felt so dejected that he began to walk, and then to crawl, with his head bent, and his arms hanging limp.

"There isn't a laugh left in the world! It's a sad, sad place, and I shall go away and play with the Polar bears and penguins. They will welcome me." He didn't really want to go to such cold places, and he glanced round to see if there was still a chance of a laugh.

On top of the hill was a windmill, with great sails lying idle. In the orchard near was a clothes-line full of washing, and a little boy ran up and down, trying to fly a kite.

The Wind tripped lightly to the house, and blew, just a little. The clothes flapped and sank and flapped again. He blew harder, and the clothes began to dance. Sheets cracked with a delicious sound, pyjamas seemed to have invisible legs, coats and petticoats were full of fat windy people who swung up and down on the line. The little

boy's kite flew up in the air, and soared on the end of the
string like a blue bird. The great sails of the windmill
with many a creak and groan began to turn, and then
went rapidly round and round.

The miller and his wife came running to the door.

"Here's the wind at last," said they, laughing to one
another. "It will grind my corn," said the miller,
joyfully.

"It will dry my washing," said his wife, as she watched
the clothes swinging in the wind.

"Look at my kite!" said the little boy. "Isn't it going
well! Like an eagle! I do like this wind," and he ran
round and round with the Wind tugging at the little
blue kite.

"Thank goodness, I've found people who like me! I
shall often come and see this laughing family. The
world's not so bad after all," said the Wind, and he
danced round and round the windmill, puffing out his
cheeks, and whistling a merry tune.

The Snow Goose

Winter was coming and the wind tore the leaves from the trees and threw them down to the ground in showers.

"The wind's in a frolic to-day. He's stripping the trees and the poor things will be cold," remarked Ann Pig. She took her little birch-besom to sweep up the leaves, but they lay so thick in the woods she had to let the wind have his own way.

Then wild gales raged from the north, and the trees were rocked and shaken.

"Let us gather firewood for the winter," said Ann, and they all ran out to collect the fallen branches, to store in the wood-shed.

Next came snow, and the soft flakes fell like feathers fluttering from the heavy clouds.

"The Old Grey Woman is plucking the white geese up yonder," said Ann, pointing to the sky. She shivered and went indoors to the fireside, but Sam Pig stood looking up, trying to see the great white birds whose feathers were falling so fast they covered the fields and woods. It was very cold and the wind cut his cheeks like a knife, so he followed Ann and sat with his brothers in the warm kitchen.

No outside work could be done. The stream was frozen, and Bill had to break a hole in the ice with a stone

to fill the kettle. There was plenty to eat, and the snow
didn't matter, for it was very cosy in the house of the four
pigs. There were strings of onions hanging in ropes from
the beams of the ceiling, and a heap of carrots under
straw in the larder. The wood-shed was piled with
potatoes and logs of wood to roast them. Tom Pig made
good warm soup every day, and Sam shook the pepper
pot over it. It was as hot as a fire, and it kept their
innards comfortable.

Away in the Fox's house it was dismal and cold, for
Mr Fox hadn't had a good meal for weeks. He had been
out every night to the rabbit warren, but the rabbits kept
close to their homes and wrapped themselves in fur
blankets and curled up in bed to keep warm. The Fox
kept watch on the pond where the water-hens and ducks
lived, but the water was frozen and the birds were wary.
They saw the tracks of the Fox in the snow, and they hid
themselves. Then the Fox went to the farm, hoping to
catch a hen for supper. The dog was loose and he
frightened the Fox away.

So the Fox got very thin with hunger, and when he
met fat little Sam Pig, who had just eaten a plateful of
hot vegetable soup, he was really angry. Sam Pig was
going to make a slide, but he stopped when he saw the Fox.

"Have you seen any geese about?" asked the Fox with
a sneer.

Sam opened wide his little blue eyes. "Geese? No,"
said he.

"I thought you might know of a few ganders, as you
know everything," scoffed the Fox, hungrily.

"The Old Grey Woman is plucking the white geese up
in the sky," said Sam, catching a snowflake and eating it.

"How do you know that?" asked the Fox with a sharp
bark.

"Here are the feathers," said Sam, innocently. "Look at them. There's a big flock of geese up there in the fields of the sky, and the Woman is plucking the feathers off and throwing them down to the earth. Ann says so, and it must be true."

The Fox was impressed.

"I could do with one of those fat geese," said he. "Where do you think they live, Sam Pig?"

"In the sky somewhere," said Sam, hesitating and looking up. "There's maybe great fields up there, and ponds and streams where the geese can swim. That's what the rain is, I 'specks. It's a pond running over and coming down on us."

"Yes," said the Fox. "That's it."

"I don't know how you will catch a goose from up there," said Sam, and he ate a few feathers thoughtfully. "Not unless the Old Grey Woman lets one slip from her knees."

"I wish she would," said the Fox fervently.

"They'll be cold if they are like this feather," said Sam, shivering.

"I don't care if they are cold as ice as long as I can get my teeth into them," said the Fox. "When they are alive they are warm. It's because the feathers have dropped such a long way on a winter's morning that they are so cold."

Sam agreed that it might be so.

"I will wait here till a goose falls from the Old Grey Woman's knee," said the Fox, and he sat down in the snow with his head raised to the sky, waiting.

Sam didn't bother to make his slide. He went home to ask all about snow geese.

When he told his brothers that the Fox was waiting for a snow goose to drop from the sky they laughed.

D

"Let's make one for him," they said. "It would be a pity if he waited for nothing, poor old Fox."

They ran to the back of the house and worked quickly, with handfuls of snow. They made a beautiful snow goose. It had a large smooth body, and a long neck and a neat head. They fixed a pair of feathery wings, ruffled and cut from the snow. Then Sam put a pair of little shiny pebbles for the eyes, and they all stood back to admire their work.

"Did you ever see such a big goose?" they whispered. "It is much more fun than making a snow pig, or even a snow man. A snow goose is a fine bird, and this is as real as life."

Sam carried it out to the field and placed it under a tree. Then he ran off to find the Fox, who was still waiting.

"Mr Fox! There's a snow goose under yonder tree. He must have flown down from the sky. Come quickly before he goes off. Oh, he is such a big one!"

The Fox shook the snow from his back and ran after Sam Pig.

"What a beautiful goose!" he cried. "Thank you, Sam Pig. It will feed us all. Thank you."

He hauled the goose on to his back and walked away. The goose was very large and the Fox was nearly covered with the snowy body. As he went through the woods the heat of his fur began to melt the snow goose, and the weight of it pressed upon him. The water turned to ice again, and stuck to his back.

"Whatever have you got there?" asked his wife as he staggered in at the door.

"A snow goose, fallen from the sky," said the Fox triumphantly. "Come, wife, and take it off my back, for it seems to have frozen on me."

So she pulled and pulled and the Fox shook himself and at last the snow goose fell to the ground.

"Why, it's only a heap of snow," cried Mrs Fox. "How foolish you are, Reynard."

"It's a snow goose from the sky, one of the geese which drop their feathers when it snows, my dear," the Fox assured her, and he pulled the goose to pieces. "Sam Pig helped me to catch it," he added.

"You are a snow goose yourself," snapped Mrs Fox. "Young Sam Pig has tricked you again."

"You are right as usual," said the Fox ruefully, looking up from the snowy heap. They both vowed vengeance on little Sam Pig as they watched the wings and the long smooth neck and the stiff little legs fall to the floor and run away like water.

Now a few days later Sam was coming back from the hen-place with a few eggs he had collected. Eggs are scarce in cold weather, and the hens had not been laying. Brother Bill fed them on warm scraps and they were so

pleased they decided to give him some eggs. They
clucked loudly to tell Sam all about it, and he ran
through the snow calling back to them.

"Sam Pig, Sam Pig. We've laid some eggs," they
shouted in their clucking voices, and Sam Pig answered,
"Thank you. Thank you, dear Fluff and Bluff, and Snow-
white and Rose-red and the rest of you."

He gathered the eggs from the warm nests, patted the
hens' soft feathers, and started back home. But to his
surprise he saw the Fox waiting for him. At first Sam
was rather frightened, remembering the snow goose, but
the Fox came smiling up to him and held out a paw.

"Shake, Sam Pig! Shake!" cried the Fox. "I want to
thank you, Sam Pig. You saved me from starvation, Sam.
Shake a paw!"

Sam put down the basket and held out his little fist,
and the Fox shook it up and down so hard that Sam was
nearly thrown off his balance. Perhaps the Fox didn't
know how much it hurt, for he kept smiling, so Sam
smiled back, although it was only a little wry smile he
gave the Fox.

"You remember that snow goose you found, Sam
Pig," said the Fox, and Sam, trembling a little, said that
he remembered.

"It was a wonderful goose, so fat, so luscious, so tender
that it melted in my mouth," said the Fox.

Sam listened, uneasily.

"Yes, Sam Pig, I shall always be grateful to you for
your kindness in telling me of the geese which the Old
Grey Woman is plucking up in the sky, and for giving
me such a fat one."

Sam's eyes widened. He could scarcely believe his ears.

"And that was not the end," continued the Fox, "for
the next day I found another snow goose, and this one

was alive. It had flown down from the sky and there it was a-sitting in the wood as tame as a hen."

"Oh my!" cried Sam Pig. "I wish I had seen it."

"It's in my wood-shed," said the Fox. "It's so tame I haven't the heart to eat it. Besides, it is laying eggs for me. Each day it lays two dozen eggs. You never saw anything like them for size. As for flavour! And shape! And goodness! Words can't tell their excellence."

The Fox spoke slowly and Sam's eyes were popping out of his head. His breath came panting in excitement, and his red tongue licked his lips. Marvels would never cease!

The Fox continued, "Those eggs are the best-tasting I ever had, with yolks all rich and whites as pure as the driven snow. We poach them, and scramble them, and make omelettes with them, and boil them, but we can't use them all up. Think of it! Two dozen eggs a day from one goose! I'm looking for another goose, Sam Pig."

Another goose! Sam Pig gasped and gazed round, also looking for another goose.

"If I can find another I shall have four dozen eggs a day, and I can give plenty away. I can give some to your family, for I don't think you get enough eggs, do you? You look very hungry, poor Sam."

"Our hens don't lay in snowy weather," said Sam. "I've got some eggs to-day, but these are the first we've had, and I am just taking them home."

The Fox picked up the basket and looked contemptuously at the brown eggs, warm from the nest.

"You should see my eggs, Sam. Four times as big as these, and full of meat. Why, one of my eggs would make an omelette for all your family, including Badger. Yes, with Badger too! These are miserable eggs, Sam. I

wouldn't give a handful of snow for eggs like these. Are
they from pigeons or wrens?"

"They are hen eggs," Sam reassured the Fox, and he
peeped at the eggs lying in the basket. It was true, they
were not as large as he had thought.

"Mr Fox," said he. "Could you—do you think you
could—er—may I see some of the eggs from the snow
goose? I've never seen a snow goose's eggs."

The Fox didn't speak for a moment. He frowned as if
he were making up his mind on some difficult matter.

"Well, as you are a friend of mine, Sam Pig, and as you
were so kind, so very kind to me, showing me the snow
goose and saving my life, I will let you have a sight of the
eggs. But mind, don't tell everybody about them, or
others will be going after the snow geese."

The Fox picked up the basket of eggs and told Sam to
follow him. They went into the wood, and the Fox
stopped by an oak-tree.

"There they are," he whispered. "She's been laying
astray again. That's another dozen. Goodness me! Three
dozen in one day! We simply can't get through them."

Sam saw a snowy nest under the tree, and in it a dozen
great oval eggs, white as snow, gleamed in the sun.

The Fox stooped and picked one up and stroked it
lovingly.

"A beautiful egg! A marvel! Cold because it was laid
by my lovely snow goose, but when I put it by the fire it
will get warm. This will make a good dinner for a
family! How lucky I am! A nest full of new-laid eggs."

He turned to Sam quickly. Sam was stooping over the
eggs. It was amazing. They were smooth and beautiful,
and white as snow. He had never imagined such big eggs,
and all laid by one snow goose!

"Sam," said the Fox softly. "Little Sam Pig. I tell you

what I will do. I will give you these eggs. Yes, I will. I will give you these eggs to take home for your brothers and Ann and Badger. Badger will be delighted. His mouth will water when he sees them! Tom will cook them and you will all have a treat."

"Oh thank you," cried Sam. "Thank you, Mr Fox. It *is* kind of you."

"Not at all," said the Fox. "You deserve them, Sam." He took the hen eggs out of the basket and dropped them casually in the snow.

"You won't want these, Sam. You won't ever want to taste hen eggs when once you've had eggs from a snow goose. There's a different flavour, an aroma, in a snow-goose egg. Your appetites will be whetted, yes, that's the word, whetted, when you get these eggs."

Sam nodded and glanced disdainfully at the little brown eggs which lay rejected in the snow. The Fox was already filling the basket with the snow-goose eggs. The basket was piled high with the glittering frosty ovals.

"If I were you, Sam," advised the Fox, as Sam lifted

the heavy basket, "if I were you I should see if you can
hatch one of those eggs, because a gosling might come
out of it. Then you would have a goose of your own. What
do you think of that?"

Sam beamed joyfully. A snow gosling! A little bird all
glittering white which would soon lay two dozen eggs.

"I will, Mr Fox," he cried. "I love goslings."

"So do I, Sam," agreed the Fox. "I see that you and
I are birds of a feather, as the old saying is. Birds of a
feather flock together. We must flock together, Sam."

Sam looked shyly at the Fox, not understanding his
words, but secretly flattered. He had always misjudged
the Fox, and really he was a kind friend.

"Put it in your bed, Sam, and it may hatch out to-night
if the bed is warm enough," said the Fox.

So Sam went home with the basket of eggs from the
snow goose, and the Fox stooped and picked up the hen
eggs and filled his pockets.

"Thank you, Sam Pig," said he softly, and he galloped
away with a smile on his face.

"Where have you been, Sam?" asked Bill, as Sam
came up the garden path with his heavy basket dragging
his arm. "You've been a long time gathering a few eggs."

Sam didn't speak, but he walked into the house and
put the basket on the table.

"Look!" he cried triumphantly. "Look, all of you.
Bill, Tom, Ann! Come here and look! Eggs from a snow
goose. Eggs laid by a snow goose."

The pigs picked up the eggs and turned them over and
sniffed at them. "Eggs from a snow goose? What do you
mean, Sam? Where are the real eggs?"

"Oh, I threw them away. These are much better.
Look at the size! One egg will be enough for all of us,
Badger too."

"Who's talking about Badger?" asked a gruff voice, and old Brock came lumbering in. "What's that you've got, Sam?"

"A dozen eggs laid by the snow goose, Brock," cried Sam, turning eagerly to the Badger. "And I'm going to put one of them in my bed to hatch into a snow gosling."

Badger picked up an egg and squeezed it in his strong paw, but it was as hard as ice.

"Eggs laid by a snow goose," he said slowly, "and brought home by the biggest goose of all."

He tossed the egg in the fire, and, with a sizzle and hiss, a stream of water ran out upon the hearth.

"Snow goose! Snow gosling!" said Badger again.

Poor Sam Pig never heard the end of that. The tale ran through the woods, so that the squirrels laughed in the tree tops and the moles chuckled under the earth. Little Sam Pig had carried a basket of snowballs home and given his hen eggs to the Fox in exchange. Snow goose! Snow goose!

🌸 Star-shine

It was winter and the snow lay thick on the fields. The trees wore white scarves on their long arms, and every twig had its spangled trimming. The roofs of the cottages were draped in smooth blankets of snow, and sharp icicles hung down from the eaves. Everybody walked softly, and even the cart-horses made no sound when they came back from work, except for the tinkling of the bells on their collars, and the jingling of their harness brasses.

At the end of the village, perched up on the side of a hill, was the shepherd's cottage, and there lived little Polly Shaw and her father. Tom Shaw was the shepherd at the farm across the valley on the opposite hill. From the cottage door there was a view of the farmstead with its fields and sheepfold and cowhouses, and Polly could stand in the porch and wave to her father minding the sheep across the stream.

Polly's mother was dead, and neighbours came in to help the shepherd to tidy the house, but when the little girl came home from school she was the small mistress who mended and darned and looked after her father. The village school was only half a mile away, up the straggling village street, and Polly never started from home until the bell which hung in the gable of the school-house was ringing and jangling. Then off she ran, leaving the cares of the little household behind. All day she did her lessons, she said her multiplication tables and her weights and measures, she read from her school book and did her sums, and sang songs with the other boys and girls. When school was over she left the merry throng who threw snowballs and slid along the black ice paths. A long row of children swooped down the slides, one following another with arms outstretched to balance, and cries of delight as their feet ground the ice. Little Polly too went down the long black slide, but when she reached the bottom of the hill she said good-bye, for she was grown-up, a child who was a home-maker, and she was proud of her trust.

So away she went to light the lamp and make up the fire and boil the kettle for tea. When her father came in he was tired, and he flung himself down in utter weariness while his little daughter cooked and washed up, as if she were a grown-up woman. But her reward came when the teacups were put in the high oak cupboard and the cloth was folded in the dresser drawer. Then Tom Shaw read aloud to her, and played on his shepherd's pipe and answered her questions and told her tales of his own childhood and her mother's, for they had been playmates at the same school in the village.

Sometimes they went to the kitchen door and waited for a signal from the farm opposite. If a lantern swung on the gate it meant that Tom Shaw was wanted that night, but when the only earthly star was the glimmer in the farmhouse the shepherd knew he could stay at home with his daughter. Then they gazed at the sky, and Tom pointed out the constellations, and told her their names.

The shepherd knew the stars, for they were his friends and companions while he guarded the sheep. They seemed to twinkle and talk to him and share his burdens. Through long winter nights he was out with the woolly beasts, tending the ewes, caring for the new-born lambs. He had a small oil stove in the lambing-hut and there he carried the little creatures and fed them when their mothers were weak, and as he went about his work the bright stars looked down. High in the deep blue of the wintry skies shone those little lamps, his own friendly lights, and when his young daughter asked their names he was glad to talk of them.

He pointed out the Square of Pegasus, the bold form of Orion the Hunter, the seven stars which make the Great Bear, and the lovely little group called the Pleiades. There was the Little Bear which prowled round the tree-tops, and the Lady Cassiopeia in her golden chair, and the fierce Dog Stars and many another. He told her how the stars revolve, and the colours change. Sometimes as they stood watching the stars, looking through an ancient telescope at the moon or the rings of Saturn, they saw other wonders. The Northern Lights lighted up the sky in flaming points. Stars shot down the great blue firmament, with a rope of gold behind them, and once they saw a comet with its long tail. Every time a shooting star fell across the sky the little girl made a wish, and since many meteorites fall in a short time for the close observer to see, she had many a wish. As the meteorites resemble each other in their long gold curves among the stars, so the wishes were the same. Polly's wish was to see her mother, who was somewhere among the stars.

One night she got out of bed and drew back the thick winter curtains. Down below was the lane and ice-covered stream, but reaching to the sky were the white hills. A glimmer of light on the distant slope showed where her father was out with the sheep. She could see the lantern moving as the shepherd carried it to the fold. Then it disappeared and she knew her father had gone into the lambing-hut, to stay for a while before he came out to his flock. He was making warm drinks for the ewes, and perhaps he would bring a small woolly black-legged lamb back to the cottage with him when he returned. He had tucked her up as usual that night, and pulled the warm blankets round her, and drawn the curtains closely across the windows. Then he had gone off to the sheep-fold and left her alone. Usually she fell asleep at once, for downstairs lay one of the dogs on guard, but this night she couldn't sleep. She stood by the window and watched the stars.

A great gold star came shooting down the sky as she stood there, and surely it was the largest meteorite ever seen. The golden rope, instead of vanishing in a second or two, hung so close to the window she felt she had only to put out a hand to catch it.

She opened the casement, and grasped it, and the rope was warm and rough with fibre, like a cart-rope at the stackyard of the farm. She shivered a moment as she climbed on the window-sill. Then out she swung, holding tight to the rope. It was just as easy as swinging on the school trapeze, out in the playground. She laughed as she leapt into the cold air. She wriggled her toes into her nightgown, and clung with her hot fists, thinking she would swing over the snowy fields and drop down upon her father at the lambing-hut.

"He'll think I'm an angel or a new-born lamb," she chuckled to herself as the golden rope swayed gently over the apple trees.

"I'll let go just as we pass over the hill," she decided. "Won't he be surprised!"

She was swept up into the air, far away from the hill-side, and the flock of ewes and the lambing-hut. Higher and higher she went towards the stars. She wasn't frightened, for the rope was comforting under her fingers, like her mother's warm clasped hand. She was carried up as easily as if she were in a basket.

At last her feet rested on a ladder, a Jacob's ladder of narrow silvery bars which went into a roof. The rope slipped from her grasp and swung in space, dangling from a ladder rung. She stepped through the door above her head and entered the starry land.

In front of her she saw a vast golden palace, with walls and turrets gleaming with light. All about were winged children playing at ball, flying and leaping, and swimming in a river of silver water.

They ran to welcome her and clustered round as if she were a new girl in the school playground.

"We've caught her, caught her," they cried, jumping round her.

"Who lives there?" she asked. "Is it the king?"

"That's the Sun's house," replied the cherub who held her hand. It fluttered its rosy wings and danced on one toe. "That's where the Sun lives! Surely you know the Sun?"

"Yes. The Sun shines all day at home, except when it rains," said Polly.

The cherub was looking curiously at her, and fat little fingers poked her shoulders and touched her nightdress.

"Where are your wings?" asked other little angels.

"I've never had any wings," replied Polly, apologetically. "I came on a golden rope."

She pointed to the door in the floor, where the ladder pushed its thin beams through, and the dangling rope was visible.

"That's the string of one of our kites," laughed the cherub. "We fly them every night. We've never caught anything before, although we have often tried to get an earth child."

"We've caught you! caught you!" echoed the others, singing like cuckoos in a wood.

"Have you really come from the earth?" they asked.

"Of course I have. I came from home, Robin Cottage, near Greeny-gate Farm. My father is shepherd there. He is out at night looking after the lambs. It's lambing-time, you know. I had a cade lamb of my own, and I fed it with a bottle of milk. There may be another for me soon. Have you sheep and lambs here?"

"No," piped the smallest cherub, and it pursed its red lips and tossed back its hair. "We've got a goat called Capella, and we've other animals whom we love. Look! Here comes one of them!"

A Great Bear came lumbering on furry feet down the slopes, and the cherub hailed him.

"Great Bear! Great Bear! Take this earth-child on your back and give her a ride round the heavens. Mind she doesn't fall off. She has no wings, poor little creature!"

"We caught her with one of the strings from our kites. Take care of her, Great Bear," said another cherub.

The shaggy animal lowered his head, and stooped his broad back. Polly grasped the long bright hair which covered him and settled herself on the thick pelt, with her feet tucked away in the warmth. Away they went, careering smoothly over the sky, with the brightly-coloured meadows under the bear's paws.

Out of the mists leapt a snowy Goat, with long twisted horns and white beard glistening with hoar frost, and golden eyes shining.

"That's Capella, our Goat star," said the Great Bear.

"I know her. She shines over the stackyard at home," said Polly. "My father showed me where she was."

"She feeds on the snow mountains. She has just come down ready for the night, when she will watch over the earth with her bright eye. Auriga, the charioteer, carries her in his arms when she is tired," said the Great Bear in his deep rumbling voice which was like thunder.

"That's like my father. He carries the tired lambs," said Polly.

"We all watch over the sleeping earth when the King Sun goes into his castle," continued the Bear. "There is no need when the Sun is driving over the broad highway which crosses the sky. He sees everything that happens

down below, but when he comes home tired at night and
his horses are stabled we take our turn."

There was a roar in the rocky heights, and a Lion
came rushing forth with flaming jaws gaping, and eyes
flashing lightnings. The wild beast ran across the heavens
and then went back to its cave.

"That's only Leo," said the Great Bear reassuringly,
as Polly clung to his fur. "He isn't fierce although he
looks so savage. Nobody minds him. He shoots his fiery
arrows to earth. Have you seen them? They are called
the Leonids."

"Yes. The shooting stars that come in November,
from the Lion. I remember," said Polly.

"Old Leo tries to frighten the horses of the Sun, but
they take no notice, and gallop along their way pulling
the chariot."

"The horses of the Sun?" asked the little girl.

"Yes. The chariot is drawn by a team of the finest
horses in the universe, fiery steeds with flashing eyes and
tossing manes of flame. Haven't you seen them cross the
sky?"

"Not horses. Only the Sun by himself," said Polly.

"The horses are there, four of them, galloping through
space, but your earth eyes are perhaps too dazzled to
see them. Some of us help to harness them at dawn, and
the Great Charioteer cracks his whip, and the doors of
heaven fly open. The grand procession rushes away at a
great speed, for it has a long way to go before it returns
to the Western door of the castle, and only a few hours
for the journey."

"We have cart-horses on the farm where my father is
shepherd," said Polly confidentially. She leaned close to
the Great Bear's ear, for there was such a rush of wind
she could hardly hear herself speak. "Are the Sun's

horses cart-horses, or racers? Can I see them up here?"

"They are race-horses, but you cannot look at them. They are in their stables, and so fierce are they that they would burn you up. I can't show you the horses, but you can see the stable doors yonder."

The Great Bear stopped near the castle, and nodded his head towards a monstrous doorway with points of fire running up from the archway which spanned it. There was a stamping of hooves and the shrill whinny of the sun-horses, but the grooms of the stable came to the door and shook their fists, and away went the Great Bear with his small burden.

They came to a starry field, where meteorites flickered like fireflies and the cherubs flew on their short curly wings. In the midst was a chair of gold and in it sat a Lady. Her eyes were soft and kind, and her voice low as she talked to the cherubs. She lifted her head when she saw the Great Bear, and the girl thought she was like her mother.

"There she is! There's the earth-child we were telling you about. She has no wings at all," cried the cherubs, and their voices were like the chattering of little birds at dawn. They rushed up to the Great Bear, and circled round his small rider.

"Be off!" growled the Bear. "Away you go!" and he shook them away as if they were pestering flies, but the Lady stretched out her arms and called to Polly.

"Come to me, earth-child. I have often heard you calling me. Come to me."

Polly dropped from the Bear's back and ran across the starry meadow. Every star was a daisy, soft under her bare feet. She climbed on the lap of the seated Lady and looked up into the beautiful face which bent towards her.

Round the Lady's neck hung a necklace of jewels, like crystals of water. Her dress was a mist of rainbow.

"You are in Cassiopeia's arms," murmured a voice, "You are safe from all evil for ever when you are here, and when you return you will look up at me and remember."

"Tell her a story. Tell her about the Moon and its lakes and mountains. Tell her about the Sun chariot. Tell her about the golden Nebulae, and all the wonderful things of heaven," cried the cherubs, circling round. They crouched at the feet of the Lady in the Chair, and the little girl stared up into the kind eyes and listened with them. Cassiopeia told one tale after another, legends of sun, earth and sky, and each was more exciting than the last.

Then the Great Bear stamped his feet and called to them.

"It's time to move on," said he. "The sun-horses are whinnying and the Grey Wolves of night are howling in the darkness. We mustn't dally here in this starry meadow. We must return."

"Good-bye, dear child," said Cassiopeia, and she took one of the gems from her necklet and hung it on Polly's breast.

"Remember what you have heard and tell the tales to the children of earth, for I love all children and would like to have them in my arms and talk to them."

She kissed her and lifted her to the high back of the Great Bear. Then she took up a harp and played music which filled the sky and echoed in all the windy places of earth, so that the poets looked up at the Chair of Cassiopeia and said, "The stars are singing to-night."

From out of the misty blue leaped a Hare, a slender animal with gilded fur and long pointed ears. After him

came two dogs with their mouths open and long jaws
gleaming.

"Oh run, Hare!" cried Polly. "Oh, they'll catch him
and kill him. Save him, Great Bear!"

"No. He is quite safe," said the Bear reassuringly.
"They will run like that for ever. The Dog Stars belong
to Orion the Hunter, and the little Hare goes across the
fields of night with the Dogs chasing him, but he knows
he cannot be caught, for that is the heavenly law. He
enjoys himself, racing over the night sky, looking down
at the quiet sleepy earth as he flees, peering at the
countries and oceans, at the lighted ships and the long
white roads, at the villages with children asleep in their
beds and the nightlights burning low. All things Lepus,
the little Hare of the sky, sees when the two dogs,
Procyon and Sirius, chase him."

"The Dog Stars," whispered Polly to herself. "Yes, I
know them well."

The Bear ambled along, and he nodded his head to
the Little Bear with the Pole Star on its head, which
came out of the wood and amiably licked Polly's foot.
Then he growled at the Dragon that lay curled in the
blue fields. The Dragon's eyes were stars which blazed
like green fires, but the Bear marched slowly onward and
Polly clung to his thick fur and looked around at the
wonderful creatures. A Swan sailed on the silver river
of the Milky Way. A Ram shook his gilded curly horns
and bent his great head to feed on the pastures. A great
Bull walked through the fields. His red eye, Aldebaran,
stared at Polly, his dewlap nearly touched the flowers,
his flanks were like molten gold. On the back of Taurus
the Bull rode one of the cherubs with a whip in its hands.
It lashed the Bull, and the whip was like the rope of a
meteorite, falling in the sky.

"It's only star-shine," cried the cherub to Polly.

Then a Giant came striding over the mountains, with feet spurning the mists and shoulders heaving the gold dust of the Nebulae. Round his waist was a jewelled belt and a short sword, and in his upheld hands a club. Even the Great Bear treated him with respect and stood aside to let him pass, but the Bull roared defiantly at Orion.

"That's Orion, the mighty Hunter," said the Bear. "He throws his club and never misses his aim. When he does this you see a star fall and one of the dark stars is driven out of heaven. The Bull tries to attack him, but Orion keeps the fierce one at bay. He waves his club on high, he raises his foot with that bright white star Rigel on the toe. Look at his belt. It is one of the marvels of the sky."

The belt glittered like gold bees, and a great jewel of a Nebula hung from it.

Orion glanced at the Great Bear, and then strode away with his hunting Dogs and the little Hare racing near him.

"He only hunts in these parts of the sky during winter months," said the Great Bear. "He visits other parts of the heavens. He travels vast distances."

As the Bear spoke there was a sound of singing, which did not come from the Harp, which played by itself in one part of the sky, nor from the Lady Cassiopeia. Polly looked round to find its source, and she spied the seven little sisters dancing in a ring.

"Those are the Seven Sisters, called the Pleiades," said the Great Bear. "They are everybody's favourites, both in heaven and earth. On the sea the sailors look out for them and call them the sailing stars, and in the fields the shepherds watch for them and call them the shepherd's stars."

"My father told me that," said Polly eagerly. "He says that once one of the stars was a lost girl, but now she has come back again."

"That's true," said the Bear. "One little sister covered her face and refused to shine, but now she is dancing as gaily as ever."

They stayed for a time to watch the dancing little Pleiades, and they listened to the sweet song.

"Would you like to join them?" asked the Great Bear. "Would you like to become a star and remain here for ever in these blue fields, dancing with our little sisters? Then your father would look up from his sheep and he would see eight little stars glittering in a bunch."

"But he would miss me," cried Polly. "Who would carry the lamb-can for feeding the young lambs? Who would light his lantern at night and welcome him home after his work in the fields? Oh no, I couldn't stay for ever up here."

There was a loud neighing from the stables of the sun-horses, and the Charioteer rolled back the doors so that the pointed flames rose high. Brilliant flashes of light came out, so dazzling that they dimmed the colour of the stars. The little Pleiades drew veils over their heads and disappeared. Orion the Hunter was already climbing the last hill with his Dogs and the little Hare. His sword gleamed, and he tossed his great head, so that the stars on his shoulders shone white in the rays that were coming from the stable doors. The sun palace was opening all its windows, and soon the Great Sun himself would step into his chariot and drive over the sky to bring light to the earth and a new day to mankind.

"Be quick!" cried the Great Bear. "You must go at once. Have you got the rope? Hold it tightly. Now away you go back to earth."

Polly slipped from his back and grasped the rope with her hands. The Great Bear held the ladder firmly and gave her a gentle push. She drifted down, down, down, with the golden light of dawn appearing above the horizon.

"Good-bye, stars," she called. "Good-bye, Great Bear, and Orion the Hunter, and the Lady Cassiopeia, and the Seven Little Sisters. I won't forget you."

"Good-bye, little earth-child," sang the stars, and their voices grew faint and they faded with the coming of the sun.

Through the open window swung Polly, and she loosed the gold rope. She climbed into bed and drew the blankets over her head. She slept so soundly she didn't hear the bleating of the newborn lamb which her father had brought home with him.

"Oh Father!" she cried, when the shepherd came upstairs to see why she slept so long. "Oh Father! I've been among the stars. I've seen them all dancing and hunting and playing up there. I've ridden on the Great Bear's back, and seen the castle of the Sun, and I've been on the Lady Cassiopeia's knee. She was like Mother, just as I remember her."

"You've been dreaming, surely," laughed her father. "You've heard my tales of the stars so often you've gone in your dreams to visit them. Now get dressed quickly and come downstairs, for I've got a weakly cade lamb I want you to look after. It's on the hearthrug before the kitchen fire."

"Oh Father! But it wasn't a dream, really!" she cried. "Look what they gave me. Look!"

Around Polly's neck hung a thin chain of spun gold like a web, and from it dropped a glittering stone which shone blue and yellow and orange, a fire-opal.

"It was a present from the Lady Cassiopeia when she told me her stories."

The shepherd took the jewel in his brown hand, and turned it to the light. It was very beautiful, a strange gem which flashed like fire, unlike anything he had ever seen.

"You must keep it in the little walnut box that was your mother's. Keep it along with her treasures," said the shepherd quietly. "It's something precious, not of this world at all. I wonder——"

He looked at his little daughter curiously.

"I wonder you didn't want to stay if they treated you so well. Didn't you want to stay there for always?" His tone was wistful, he seemed half afraid.

"No." She flung her arms round his neck and held him close, smelling the rough familiar smell of sheep and earth and straw.

"No, I wanted to come back to earth, to look after you and the lambs and the sheep dogs," she whispered, burying her nose in his black hair.

She lifted her head and looked deep in his searching eyes.

"I shall never forget the tales I heard, nor the sights I saw. No, never."

"I'm glad you didn't forget me, alone down here, Polly," said the shepherd and he went downstairs, clumping slowly in his heavy boots. The sound of the bleating lamb came through the floor to the girl. She dressed quickly and ran down to join the little company, her father, the sheep dogs, and the new-born lamb. To these she told all I have told you, and more besides.

The Seven Sleepers

Snow fell softly on the world, covering the fields and hedges with a big white blanket. In the sky the Moon peered this way and that to find the house of the Seven Sleepers. At last she saw a little green cottage under the holly tree in Big Wood, nestling so close to the dark trunk that its thatched roof touched the low, shining branches, and its small chimney pressed against the prickly leaves.

She gazed curiously at its tightly shut windows, and the door with its brass knocker, all dull with the rain and snow. Then she flashed her lantern through the end window, and saw the nose of a red squirrel who lay curled up in bed. Squirrel started slightly when the light fell on her and pulled the sheet over her face.

"Safe as moonshine," said the Moon, and she peeped through all the little windows in a row under the eaves. In each room somebody lay asleep, and the Moon laughed to herself.

As she stared in at the tiny room with delicate blue curtains, the room which was so small she could scarcely get her moonbeam inside, she heard a slight sound, and a strange being came through the wood.

His face was glowing with light, and his kind brown eyes were like the eyes of a young fawn. On his shaggy back he carried a sack, and twisted round his short horns was a wreath of mistletoe. He danced along on his cloven hoofs, and played on thin reed pipes the sweetest music the Moon had ever heard.

The Moon bowed when she saw him, and shielded her lantern, for no light was needed when Pan the friend of animals was there.

"You are first," said Pan, resting the sack on the snow. "Are they all asleep in there?" and he pointed to the windows.

"Yes, Your Majesty," replied the Moon, "but Squirrel is restless."

"She always is," laughed Pan, straightening out his broad shoulders, and stamping his hoofs on the ground. "She always is. The least sound, and out of bed she hops. She is the only wakeful one of the Seven Sleepers, and when she comes out in the Winter, woe betide her if I am not near!"

"Is Your Majesty honouring them with a visit?" asked the Moon.

"Of course," answered Pan. "It's Christmas Eve, you know. Animals as well as men must have their joy. I cannot do much nowadays, but this is one of the privileges left to me."

"It's cold for Your Majesty," said the Moon, flashing her lantern up and down, on the trees and hills and distant villages, where the dogs howled when they saw her. "Shall I ask the Sun to hurry up and warm things a little?"

"Ah! no," cried Pan quickly. "I must work at night now, there are too many eyes when the Sun awakes."

He slung his pipes round his hairy neck, pushed open the door and entered the cottage.

"It was a piece of luck to see him," cried the Moon to herself. "He slides along in the shadows so softly no one knows he is there, except for the sound of his pipes. I'll wait till he comes out again." And she pulled a cloud over her face and had a nap.

Pan busied himself in the kitchen for a few moments, and then ran noiselessly upstairs.

On the landing were seven little doors.

He listened, and a smile of contentment spread over his wise old face.

Little grunts and squeaks, sighs and shuffles, came from all the bedrooms, as the sleepers dreamed of summer days, of green hills, and shallow streams, of flowery meadows and soft wet bogs. A hundred visions ran through their heads, and each one lived again in the country of his heart's desire, whilst Pan stood outside in the passage breathing happiness into all the little hearts beating within.

But there was no time to lose. He gently turned a door knob and walked into Squirrel's room. There she lay, curled up with her bushy tail over her feet, smiling in her sleep, and at the foot of the bed hung her red stocking.

Pan dipped into his bag and pulled out a pair of curly-wool slippers, white and soft, woven from the fleece of a mountain lamb. He pushed them deep in the stocking, and then skipped lightly out of the room. Squirrel dreamed of waving beech trees, and great oaks, and little nut trees laden with brown nuts, but she did not know who had brought her the dream.

Then the god went into the next room, where, on a round, soft, leafy bed lay Snake, coiled in a ring, with her head on a pillow of grass. From a hook in the ceiling hung her long black stocking, for although she had no feet, she possessed a useful stocking, which she kept for sore throats, or Christmas Eve, or for a portmanteau when she was going on a long journey.

Into it Pan slipped a green silk dress, all frills and spickles and speckles.

"She'll want a new dress next Spring," said he, as he tiptoed out of the room on his pointed hoofs, and left the Snake dreaming of shadowy green glades, and thick wet grass, with deep hiding-places.

Dormouse slept in the next room. He was such a jolly chubby little fellow that Pan stood watching him for a precious minute. He lay in his cot with the eiderdown pulled up to his chin, grunting softly as he dreamed of a round nest under the hedge, with seven tiny babies in it.

At the foot of the cot hung a brown sock, and Pan put a little fur waistcoat inside it.

"Keep him warm when he wakes up, the young fellow," said he, and he touched the small head lovingly, and gently closed the door.

Hedgehog's room was next. He lay in a ball at the top of the blankets, with a pink stocking tied to one of his prickles.

"He doesn't mean to lose it," laughed Pan, as he untied it and dropped inside a pearly knife with two blades and a corkscrew. Then he tied it up again and looked at the gently breathing animal.

"That's a fine present for a Hedgehog, for life will be none too easy for him," and Hedgehog dreamed of a hawthorn hedge, thick and leafy, with wood sorrel and sweet-smelling ferns growing at its roots, and big white eggs laid by some stray hen in a hollow.

"That's four," sighed Pan, as he stepped into the next room.

Frog slept there, in a bed woven of reeds, with a wet sheet tied round his chin. He snored and snored and kicked his little legs about, but when Pan came near he lay very still, as if he felt the presence of the Animals' Friend.

Pan took a pair of skates from his sack and put them in the green stocking which lay on the floor where Frog had kicked it.

"You can skate on dry land if there isn't any ice," he whispered, "and some time you will be saved from an enemy."

And the Frog smiled as he dreamed of murmuring streams, and lily ponds, of hard round pebbles, and soft silky mud.

"Now for Snail," said Pan, as he opened the door next to Frog's. There, on a little white sheet, lay a shell, and inside it was Snail, fast asleep. But she had not forgotten to hang out her tiny grey stocking when she went to bed three months ago.

Pan brought out of his sack a necklace, made of dewdrops, the colour of rainbows.

"Ha!" he chuckled. "Won't little Snail startle them when she wears her jewels!"

There was only one room left, but that was his favourite, and Pan loved to see the neat beauty of that room. He opened the very small door at the end of the passage, and crept in on his shaggy knees, bending his horns to the ground to get through the doorway.

Such a warm cosy room was Bee's! Its walls were hung with blue silk, and its blue velvet carpet was rich as a pansy petal. On the smallest bed in the world slept Bee, with a patchwork quilt over her furry body, and her head on a feather pillow as big as a pea. Tiny, tiny snores came from the bed, and her wings moved up and down as she breathed. But as Pan entered she dreamed of the wide moors with purple heather, of the great lime-trees with golden flowers, of hedges with wild roses and honey-suckle, and a flicker of a smile crossed her face.

Pan searched for her stocking, but it was so small that even his quick bright eyes nearly missed it. There it hung, all feathery and fluffy, on one of the bed knobs. He could only just get a wee pot of honey into it.

"Good Luck to you, little Bee," he cried, as he crept back into the passage and shut the small door.

Downstairs he went, carrying his sack on his shoulder, and out into Big Wood, where the Moon was waiting to see him again. He put his pipes to his lips and played a tune, and the stars leaned down to watch him, and the trees bent their heads to listen.

"Good-bye, Seven Sleepers," he cried. "A Happy Christmas, and Good Hunting in the Spring."

Then away he went, to carry bundles of hay to the cows in their stalls, sieves of corn to the horses in the stables, and comfort and cheer to all the animals who were waiting for him in the byres.

The Moon leaned through the branches of the holly-tree, and peered at the sleeping animals.

"Good night, Seven Sleepers. Sleep well until Spring comes to waken you," she called, and then she sailed away to meet Orion the Hunter with his two dogs, who waited for her in the starry spaces.

The Queen Bee

The Queen Bee, with her little gold crown on her head, buzzed through the open window of the dining-room to the sugar-bowl on the table. She tasted a bit, and nodded approvingly. Then she broke off a small piece and carried it out into the sunshine, to the palace on the patch of grass under the rose bushes.

She summoned her Prime Minister.

"Taste this," she commanded, holding out the sugar.

He bent his proud head, and gently licked the glistening morsel.

"Your Majesty!" he exclaimed. "It is frozen sweetness. It is crystal honey. May I ask where Your Majesty found it?"

The ladies-in-waiting crowded round, peeping over each other's shoulders, their soft eyes bright, and their delicate wings neatly folded at their sides. They listened breathlessly to the Queen's reply.

"I found it in a dark cave across the garden," said she. "There is a store, nuggets as large as flowers, piled in a silver bowl, on a stretch of grass as white as snow."

The youngest lady-in-waiting pressed forward, and eagerly cried:

"Couldn't we all go, Your Majesty, and bring back a supply for the needs of the people in winter?"

"Wisely spoken," said the Queen, smiling.

She rang a little bell to call her subjects. From clover field and lime-tree, from rose bush and hedgerow, they flew in and surged round her in a black mass.

"Go to the dark cave, my people," she commanded, "and bring the white sweetness to the palace. Fear nothing, your swords will not be needed, for the giants who live there will flee from you."

They each took a little bag from the palace walls, and fastened it to their legs. Then they went out of the big front door, and down the sloping drive, pushing and jostling with their tiny soft feet, rubbing their wings against each other, nudging, whispering, laughing and talking.

They rose in the air and flew in a straight line across the sunny garden, over the sweet peas and poppies, past the mignonette and marigolds, to the open window of the house.

The sugar-bowl lay on the table, and a maid stood near with a tray.

"Mercy on us!" she cried, running to the door. "The bees are swarming in the house," and she ran out of the room into the study where her master sat writing.

"What is it?" he asked, frowning.

"Please sir, the dining-room is full of a swarm of bees," she exclaimed.

"Don't bother me! Just leave them alone, and they'll go away," he said impatiently banging on his desk.

But when she timidly put her nose round the door, there was nothing left, not even a lump of sugar. The bowl was quite empty!

The Queen sat in her parlour, combing and brushing her hair. She put on her crown when she heard the rush of wings outside, and went down to meet her subjects.

She climbed on her throne, and her ladies-in-waiting stood round her. Each bee brought a load of sugar and emptied it out before her.

Soon a great white heap lay on the floor of the throne room.

The Queen clapped her hands, and a party of white-

capped little cooks ran in. They stored the sugar in the
pantry, and sealed it in the hexagonal cupboards with the
royal wax.

But still the bees surged up and down the floor, and
the Prime Minister whispered to the Queen: "Your loyal
subjects want a speech, Your Majesty."

"Speech! Speech!" buzzed the bees.

The Queen rose, towering above them.

"My good people," she began. "We thank you for
this supply of sweetness for the cold months of winter
which are before us. If now some of you will get the
juices of fruits, we will make the honey beloved of our
ancestors, the bees who lived in the Golden Age."

"Hip, hip, hurrah! Long live the Queen!" shouted the
bees.

A party of them went off with little vessels under their
wings, to rifle the fruit-trees. They sucked the juices from
the purple plums and squeezed the richness from the
blackberries. They took the sweetness from the yellow
pears and the ripe apples. Only the scarlet crab-apples
and the little hard sloes they left untouched.

The Queen donned a white apron and went into the
big kitchen, where the kitchen-maids stood ready with
silver pans. She emptied the juice into the pans, and
the busy workers carried sugar from the stores and poured
it over the juice. Then the cooks ran out of doors with all
the pans, and left them in the sunshine for an hour,
whilst a bodyguard marched round and round, to keep
off the enemy earwigs and ants, who tried to dip their
fingers in the sweet-smelling syrup.

When the air was filled with fragrance, and the tiny
silken bubbles burst in the pans, the Queen came to look.

"Take it in and store it in the cupboards," she said,
and a hundred cooks emptied it in the cells.

The Queen watched them seal it all up before she took off her apron and returned to affairs of State.

One day, when the cold winds of winter blew, and the flowers had long since disappeared from the garden, the Queen sent the youngest lady-in-waiting to the store-room with a crystal cup and a tiny gold knife. She cut the wax from one of the cells and drew out a rich red liquid.

The Queen drank first, and passed the cup round among her Court. As each bee drank, she smiled and cried, "Wonderful! A miracle!" and passed on the cup to the next eager neighbour.

"What is the name of this marvellous food, please, Your Majesty?" asked the Prime Minister.

"It is the Syrup of the Bees," answered the Queen, proudly, "and it has not been made for a thousand years. But it is a food which must only be used in a time of necessity, for it will not change with age." So she sealed up the syrup again, and returned to her bedroom.

Now that year the Snow Queen decided to reign in England. She brought her ice-maidens with her, and her courtiers with their long spear-like icicles. They locked up the earth for many months, so that nothing could come forth. With strong ice bands, stronger than steel, they bound the trees so that no leaf could get out, and they fastened up the earth, so that flowers and plants were imprisoned.

The Queen Bee looked from her window at the white garden, and waited for that feeling and scent in the air which would tell her spring had come. But spring hammered in vain at the doors of the woods and fields.

A few scouts left the palace and flew over the meadows, seeking for flowers; but they never returned, they were frozen to death.

Then the Prime Minister visited the Queen.

"Your Majesty," said he, "there is no food for the people. They have eaten up all the honey, and the pieces of sweetness we stored for them when the days were sunny. They are clamouring for bread. But the cold winds blow, and the ice binds the flowers, and famine faces us."

Then the Queen knew the time had come to unseal the precious Syrup of the Bees. She gave the rich crimson food to her ladies-in-waiting, and they carried it to the swarms of impatient hungry bees, who surged over the palace floors.

Their strength returned, their eyes sparkled. Every day they were fed, for a little of the syrup went a long way, and every day their wings grew firmer, ready for their long flights when they could escape from the hive.

At last the Sun conquered the Snow Queen, and she fled back to her kingdom at the North Pole.

Then the Queen Bee ordered the porters to open wide the palace door. Out flew the swarm of bees, strong and well, with their baskets on their thighs, to seek the fresh honey from the young flowers which had feebly pushed their way through the earth.

But the Queen went to her parlour with her youngest lady-in-waiting, and there she played a little secret tune on her virginal, to welcome the arrival of the poor late spring.